PRAISE FOR M. L. BUCHMAN

A fabulous soaring thriller.

> — *TAKE OVER AT MIDNIGHT,* MIDWEST
> BOOK REVIEW

Meticulously researched, hard-hitting, and suspenseful.

> — *PURE HEAT,* PUBLISHERS WEEKLY,
> STARRED REVIEW

Expert technical details abound, as do realistic military missions with superb imagery that will have readers feeling as if they are right there in the midst and on the edges of their seats.

> — *LIGHT UP THE NIGHT,* RT REVIEWS, 4 1/2
> STARS

Buchman has catapulted his way to the top tier of my favorite authors.

> — FRESH FICTION

Nonstop action that will keep readers on the edge of their seats.

M L. Buchman's ability to keep the reader right in the middle of the action is amazing.

The only thing you'll ask yourself is, "When does the next one come out?"

The first...of (a) stellar, long-running (military) romantic suspense series.

I knew the books would be good, but I didn't realize how good.

Buchman mixes adrenalin-spiking battles and brusque military jargon with a sensitive approach.

— PUBLISHERS WEEKLY

13 times "Top Pick of the Month"

— NIGHT OWL REVIEWS

Tom Clancy fans open to a strong female lead will clamor for more.

— *DRONE*, PUBLISHERS WEEKLY

Superb! Miranda is utterly compelling!

— *BOOKLIST*, STARRED REVIEW

Miranda Chase continues to astound and charm.

— BARB M.

Escape Rating: A. Five Stars! OMG just start with *Drone* and be prepared for a fantastic binge-read!

— READING REALITY

The best military thriller I've read in a very long time. Love the female characters.

— *DRONE*, SHELDON MCARTHUR,
FOUNDER OF THE MYSTERY BOOKSTORE,
LA

THE DISAPPEARANCE CIPHER

A DILYA'S SECRET DOG FORCE NOVEL

M. L. BUCHMAN

SIGN UP FOR M. L. BUCHMAN'S NEWSLETTER TODAY

The Emily Beale Universe
(military romantic suspense)

The Night Stalkers
MAIN FLIGHT
The Night Is Mine
I Own the Dawn
Wait Until Dark
Take Over at Midnight
Light Up the Night
Bring On the Dusk
By Break of Day
Target of the Heart
Target Lock on Love
Target of Mine
Target of One's Own
NIGHT STALKERS HOLIDAYS
Daniel's Christmas*
Frank's Independence Day*
Peter's Christmas*
Christmas at Steel Beach
Zachary's Christmas*
Roy's Independence Day*
Damien's Christmas*
Christmas at Peleliu Cove

Henderson's Ranch
Nathan's Big Sky*
Big Sky, Loyal Heart*
Big Sky Dog Whisperer*
Tales of Henderson's Ranch*

Shadow Force: Psi
At the Slightest Sound*
At the Quietest Word*
At the Merest Glance*
At the Clearest Sensation*

White House Protection Force
Off the Leash*
On Your Mark*
In the Weeds*

Firehawks
Pure Heat
Full Blaze
Hot Point*
Flash of Fire*
Wild Fire
SMOKEJUMPERS
Wildfire at Dawn*
Wildfire at Larch Creek*
Wildfire on the Skagit*

Delta Force
Target Engaged*
Heart Strike*
Wild Justice*
Midnight Trust*

Emily Beale Universe Short Story Series

The Night Stalkers
The Night Stalkers Stories
The Night Stalkers CSAR
The Night Stalkers Wedding Stories
The Future Night Stalkers

Delta Force
Th Delta Force Shooters
The Delta Force Warriors

Firehawks
The Firehawks Lookouts
The Firehawks Hotshots
The Firebirds

White House Protection Force
Stories

Future Night Stalkers
Stories (Science Fiction)

ABOUT THIS TITLE

WHEN ONE OF THE NATION'S TOP SPIES DISAPPEARS, HOW CAN Dilya find her? Or should she?

Dilya Stevenson, nanny and dog sitter to the First Family, always trusts herself, her dog, and her mentor—first, second, and third. Everyone else stands outside that circle.

But when her retired-spymaster mentor disappears, Dilya and the First Dog can't find her alone. To save her mentor's future, she must reconnect with her own past.

Originally published as a five-story series: "The Race Begins," "The Library Trail," "The Catalog Message," "The Railway Code," and "The Two-Dog Solution."

PART ONE

THE RACE BEGINS

1

DILYA TRIED TO BREATHE BUT HER MOUTHFUL OF DOG FUR made it hard.

She didn't care one bit and squeezed Zackie harder. The Sheltie, which looked like a knee-high, brown-and-white collie, wiggled in her arms, pressing into the hug. Tears wasn't something she did, a couple times close but...no. Not since her parents had been gunned down in front of her, leaving her to survive in the high Hindu Kush Mountains of Afghanistan as a child. Not even the day she'd found her new family.

"I'm going to miss you so much."

Zackie made a happy noise in reply as if Dilya wasn't about to rip out the dog's heart by leaving. She'd been the official dog sitter for the First Family since they'd been the Second Family and brought a fresh-weaned puppy to DC.

Now she was leaving, and the truth was that Zackie wasn't hers. The dog belonged to the President's wife.

"Why are you going to miss her?"

Dilya startled and did her best to wipe her eyes on Zackie's long fur. Air Force One was such a pain—there was no way to be alone on this plane. She'd come down to the lower cargo deck to walk Zackie as she often did on flights. This wasn't a long flight, DC to the Tennessee family farm, but Zackie was a Sheltie and didn't have a calm mode unless commanded to.

Then everything had caught up with her until she'd collapsed on the bottom step of the stairs and hauled Zackie into her lap. She should have moved out of the line of sight from the main deck. But now that she'd been caught, she couldn't ignore First Lady Anne Darlington-Thomas.

Her catching breath *might* be masked by the engine's roar, unbuffered by sound insulation at this level.

"I'm sorry," she kept her voice under tight control as she looked up and opened her eyes wider so that the water of her near-tears was spread out across her eyeballs rather than squeezed out to trickle down. "I quit."

The soft smile on Anne's face fractured than disappeared. She nudged Dilya to the side and then sat on the step beside her. It wasn't proper, but there was no use telling the First Lady that. She'd grown up on a Tennessee farm. Being from one of the leading farm families of the South had never stopped her from mucking out her horse's stall.

"Well, it's about time."

Dilya had already known how this conversation would go—and this wasn't it.

"Oh, we'll miss you and never find a nanny like you."

"Mirabella *tries.*" Dilya knew her dry tone could soak up the Potomac River but couldn't quite mask the sarcasm.

"Yes, she is *good,*" the First Lady matched her tone for tone. "We needed her when you started college."

"But not as good as me?"

"Three quarters at the most. Trust me. That's the best

anyone could ever be." Anne's humor crashed Dilya's mood even further. She'd never been more than okay as a nanny despite her best efforts; there were too many enticing distractions. Conscientious? Sure. Even thought she had it down. Until she saw Mirabella playing with the White House toddlers; little-kid-awesome must be in her DNA.

"I'm sorry."

Anne bumped her own shoulder against Dilya's in a friendly fashion. She still wasn't used to being two inches taller than the First Lady. That was simply...wrong.

"Wait! What did you mean *it's about time?*"

"I wondered when you'd get back to that. Dilya, you were rescued by the Night Stalkers in Afghanistan when you were, perhaps, eleven?"

She shrugged. Dilya had never corrected anyone about their guesses of her age. She'd always pretended ignorance, as if a kid didn't know their own age. She remembered how confidently the First and Second Kids both had known when they were *free year ol'*. When she'd been a war orphan recently rescued by the Night Stalkers, she'd found it an advantage to appear younger than her actual nine—young enough to be easily ignored and forgotten. But her rescuers hadn't, they'd adopted her instead and become her second set of parents.

Now it was better for people to think her older. Normal girls didn't graduate top ten at Georgetown University in three years with double majors before they were twenty. School had been the easy part. Living in—and paying attention to—everything around her at the White House, had taught her more than most of her poli-sci or international affairs professors knew themselves.

That had left her plenty of time to pursue Miss Watson's extracurricular coursework. Her assignments had been far more challenging than anything a university could put together. Of course, what chance did a mere professor have when compared to one of America's foremost spymasters.

"You came to the White House seven years ago at fourteen—" *not yet twelve* "—as nanny to the First Lady and soon after as my dog sitter when I married the Vice President."

Dilya nodded, the rest of that was accurate enough.

"You grew up taking care of our families. It's time for you to go out and find your own life."

"I will miss them." Her glance up and forward included the First and Second families' children currently napping in the President's private cabin.

"But they're only four and you can't be a nanny the rest of your life," Anne agreed.

"I wish I could be different. Somehow—"

"Not you," Anne cut her off. "Mirabella could. She may be with us for years, but not you. I do have one question though."

Dilya held Zackie tightly in her lap. There were two likely questions and she hated the answer to both. *Can I have my dog back and—*

"Why now?"

And Dilya felt the abyss open again.

This morning.

A bare room that hadn't been bare in all her years at the White House.

Mechanical Room 043 in the White House Residence's lowest subbasement had become the most reliable touchstone of her life, perhaps even more than her adoptive parents.

There lay the hidden secret at the core of the government. Beyond the non-descript steel door lay the most complete library of actual spy craft anywhere. An elegant sitting room hidden behind one of the tightly packed bookcases. And the master spy who had sat at its center, protecting the government that thought her long dead.

She hid her face once again in Zackie's fur.

This morning she and Zackie had followed one of the many circuitous routes she'd developed to reach the Residence's deepest level unobserved—only to find it bare. The steel door, that only ever unlocked the moment before her hand touched the handle, had stood ajar.

Inside...no desk. No shelves of books. The bookcases that had hidden the sitting room behind were swung wide. No brocade armchairs. No portrait wall displaying the greatest female spies of history. No sweet pea decorated tea set or Snoopy doghouse biscuit jar with treats for Zackie.

Dilya wondered if she'd hallucinated all her time here, or was hallucinating now when it appeared to be a barren wasteland. She'd doubted until she saw Zackie cock her head plaintively at where the Snoopy jar had rested on a small rosewood table. The echo of her whisper of Miss Watson's never-spoken aloud name yet another proof this was real. The familiar rush of dishwasher water through the overhead pipes confirmed that at least something here hadn't changed.

Swept clean.

She'd checked every corner, the top edges of the door and bookcases, the back edge of every shelf she could remove. Rubbed her hands raw across every surface seeking a coded message of some kind. In *Dune,* the Lady Jessica had found a secret message encoded by bumps on a plant leaf. No plants. She'd even scrounged up a blacklight to no avail. Inside the door frame, outside. Nothing.

Zackie, when given the command to seek, hadn't managed more than two steps past the door of the room before losing the scent.

At a loss, they'd had to race upstairs by the most direct route and had barely caught the helo from the South Lawn to Andrews, committing the major sin—at least in the standing Marine Corps guardsman's eyes—of boarding *after* the President.

Miss Watson was gone.

And to the best of her knowledge, no one at the White House knew she'd ever been there. Someone must, but she had no idea who. Actually, she knew four people who knew her. They'd met her through Dilya, but maybe they knew things about Miss Watson that she didn't.

You need to exceed me, child—Miss Watson was the only one still allowed to call her that. *Think in teams, not individuals. It is my one great failing, don't let it be yours.*

Were her old high school friends a team? No. But they'd been friends. A close-knit group of misfits, all exceptional in their own way. Lost one by one as they attended different colleges. In touch but nothing like they'd been.

Task One. Get away from the known. If someone had taken out Miss Watson, they'd watch every known path for repercussions and aftershocks.

She looked at Anne, her eyes now dry. The fear ran too deep for tears to flow against the pressure. The engines dropped in tone, the nose pitched down, and she could hear the pilot announcing the start of the descent.

"I'm sorry. It just has to be now."

Anne's look said that she'd have been better off making up a lie that they could both laugh off as obvious, but there wasn't one in her. After studying her for a long minute— Dilya knew better than to turn away and prove she had

secrets not even the First Lady could be trusted to know—
Anne reached out to scritch Zackie's ears.

The Sheltie lolled her head backward over Dilya's arm
and sighed happily.

And here came the second intolerable question.

"Have you seen the girls with Zackie's litter?"

And again Anne was never quite what she expected.

They were impossible to miss and, despite the inner
churning of her current turmoil threatening to drown out
Air Force One's engines, it was equally impossible not to
smile.

The First and Second Ladies had given birth only weeks
apart, their girls were now four. And the former First Lady's
daughter was a terribly sophisticated seven. Whenever they
were at the White House, all three girls melted into puddles
of goo that were inseparable from the little fluffballs. At
three months, the Sheltie puppies were not so little
anymore.

"We're going to give a puppy to each one," Anne
continued.

"And the fourth?" It would be a lot of work to train a
puppy to Zackie's level. Over the last seven years she'd had
plenty of help from the Secret Service dog handlers and
every military war dog handler Dilya could pin down. But it
would be wonderful if she could have one of Zackie's
brood for—

"I think that I'll keep it for myself. It would be a shame
to separate them."

Dilya nodded, keeping her face as passive as she'd
done those first days when the Night Stalkers were trying
to figure out what to do with the war orphan they'd
rescued.

Anne scratched Zackie's ears again. "She has ended up

being far more *your* dog than mine or the President's. You two take care of each other."

Dilya could only gawk as Anne leaned forward to kiss Zackie on top of the snout and then herself on the temple.

Long gone before she could recover, Anne left behind only the light scent of her lovely honey-scented perfume.

2

THE PLANE LANDED IN TRI-CITIES AIRPORT, NORTHEAST Tennessee. A regional airport barely big enough to deserve the name, but it could handle the big jet and lay less than twenty miles from the Darlington family farm.

She faded from the exodus by laying low and deplaning along with the baggage handlers into the hot summer afternoon—her stomach still too scrunched to take advantage of lunch on the hour-long hop from DC. Anne's smile and her hand pressed against the window of the Marine One helicopter were the only signs that anyone had missed her from the typical entourage headed to the farm.

After moving far enough away from Air Force One for her phone to drop the plane's wireless network and hook up to a local cell tower, she placed the call she hadn't dared try on-board where everything was monitored. A random cell call? Not so much.

Still, she pulled up a VPN and chose an end-to-end encrypted app as a precaution.

Major Emily Beale, supposedly retired, answered on the second ring. "Dilya! How are you?" She sounded pleased.

Dilya had never gotten used to the idea that such an amazing person could be one of her friends. The first female Special Operations helicopter pilot for the 160th Night Stalkers—so good they couldn't keep her out. And that was before she'd been awarded numerous medals, fought wildfires, or now worked for Miss Watson. Dilya also liked it that Miss Watson called Emily *my child* as well.

"I'm okay."

"I see. What's going on?" One of the problems with Emily was that Dilya had never been able to hide anything from her—ever. On the other hand, being the ultimate female warrior, Emily always plunged straight into the business at hand without wasting time, which was a relief. There was a brief rattle of keys, "And where are you?"

Dilya ignored the second question, she'd long since disabled all location services on this device. She didn't know if even Emily could break through to find out where she actually was, not that it mattered—yet.

"Have you spoken with our friend lately?"

"Hmmm... That narrows it down not in the slightest." Which was true. But not.

"*Our* friend," Dilya prompted. *My parents* were Emily's friends but she would have called them that. *Your friend* might include the former President turned Secretary of State because they'd grown up as neighbors, or perhaps Michael Gibson since he'd retired from commanding Delta Force. *Our friend,* combined with the fact that she hadn't said a name outright, would be Secret Service Agent Frank Adams or...

"Oh. No, I haven't. Not for several weeks."

Dilya had seen Miss Watson four days ago. She wished there was a wall to lean against for support and her stomach convinced her that skipping lunch had been the right choice. She scanned around to make sure that no one but Zackie lurked nearby. They were alone on the tarmac, at the edge of the security perimeter that now encircled the 747.

Emily waited.

"The room is empty," Dilya kept it simple.

"Empty?" Not in doubt but as if the word was blown out of her.

"Nothing. I checked every surface." She hoped Emily could keep following her meaning.

"Hold please," her tone now almost mechanical. But she didn't mute her phone.

Dilya could hear it thunk down on the desk, followed by the harsh rattle of computer keys. Then a brief squeal followed by a ringing that indicated a military-grade encrypted phone. More key rattle.

It was three full minutes before Emily came back on. "I'm going to send Michael to you. He—"

"No. He leaves too big a wake."

Emily laughed. "You don't know Michael then."

Your friend, Colonel Michael Gibson, had been Delta Force's most skilled warrior, might still be even though he'd retired. But if someone had removed Miss Watson, they would be expecting such a player to surface and be watching for him.

Emily and Michael had been the first step along the action-team chain from Miss Watson.

They'd know little or nothing about the intelligence gathering arm, which was Dilya's specialty, mostly—partly anyway. Dilya didn't know what she was anymore.

Or the political arm.

Or... Dilya wondered how much else she didn't know about.

She kept her silence, letting Emily figure it out.

There was a long pause before Emily admitted defeat with a soft sigh.

"What are you thinking?" She'd have figured out why not to send Michael almost immediately, spending the rest of the silence cranking through successively less useful alternatives exactly as Dilya had.

Maybe not *exactly*.

One thing that Michael and her adoptive mom had taught her, never come at a problem head-on. Emily was a Spec Ops warrior. She and Dad had gone through West Point then flown together. They couldn't help that. Delta Force had trained Michael to come at problems sideways.

Kee had grown up on the streets of East LA and was now a top sniper for the Hostage Rescue Team—Mom could do *anything*. Except she didn't know about Miss Watson. It was beyond weird to think that she, Dilya, could do something neither Emily nor Kee could.

"I need to get moving."

"Be—" Emily caught herself before saying *careful*. She knew Dilya would be better at that than even she herself would in this type of situation. After all, Dilya had been trained by both the Night Stalkers warriors and a top spymaster. "—in touch."

"Okay." Dilya hung up.

Unless something went truly sideways, that wasn't going to happen until this was resolved. Once Emily figured out that truth, Dilya hoped that it wouldn't make her too angry.

3

Northeastern Tennessee. Her traveling backpack and —*her* dog! She knelt to give Zackie another big hug. The gesture earned her a happy sigh from the depths of the Sheltie's nap on the warm tarmac—she was a complete heat-glutton despite her thick fur.

Never in a thousand dog years had Dilya expected such a gift. Anne Darlington-Thomas was the best person ever. Or...kinda. In the same top-tier category as Mom and Emily anyway. Someday she'd find a way to pay that back, even if it was only working to keep the First Lady safe without her knowledge.

Dilya straightened.

First task? Think!

Yes, Miss Watson.

She'd gathered her initial data: empty room, and the fact that Emily didn't know. That also meant that Lauren and Michael didn't know either as they also lived on and worked from Henderson's Ranch in Montana. Others had traveled through the covert sub-basement domain, but only briefly as far as Dilya knew. Three Secret Service dog handlers, the

White House chocolate chef, and the driver of the Presidential limo. But only Dilya had remained attached to her across all of the last eight years—at least as far as she knew.

But what did she know? *Actually* know? Had Miss Watson hidden other on-going relations?

Surely. But over the last four years, Dilya had come to know more and more about what passed across Miss Watson's desk and had heard only the least of hints about other people.

One of Air Force One's stray Secret Service agents strolled over. "Hey, Dilya. Miss the Marine One flight to the ranch? You can hop in with the luggage." He waved a hand toward a pair of black Suburban SUV's with tinted glass.

So much for departing unnoticed.

The main motorcade had left as soon as the helos were airborne and would soon be occupying the lower barn on the Darlington Farm—out of sight and instantly ready.

"No, I'm good thanks."

He eyed her, the baggage vehicles, then her again. Finally he shrugged and moved on with a wave.

Almost anonymous.

Now that she'd stopped long enough to think, her next move—other than getting out of the known paths—was obvious.

She snapped her fingers.

Zackie popped up from her nap and trotted along beside her.

4

Kimberlee Walker puzzled at the message, *Miss Baker*, from an unlisted number.

She knew who that was, of course. Even if Miss Baker wasn't buried less than a hundred meters from where she was standing, Kimberlee couldn't be her father's daughter and *not* know. Like his pa before him, Senator Jerome Walker had been deeply involved in the US space program before, unlike Grandpa, turning to politics.

The Marshall Space Flight Center had loomed so large in her childhood that it still mystified her when people didn't know that NASA's largest center wasn't Houston, Canaveral, or Vandenberg—but here in Huntsville, Alabama.

And for the visitors? The US Space and Rocket Center: combined museum, astronautics adventure park, and the home of Space Camp. Her summer job through high school hadn't been barista or grocery clerk, it had been working with SC kids on engineering skills and space-training experiences. She could stabilize the multi-axis spin simulator faster than any kid yet because she'd been doing it since she could fit in the chair.

Dad wanted her to go to space. She'd always assumed that an astronaut application was in her future.

Now, she didn't know. She'd thought it was gone but all of a sudden it wasn't, which meant—

Miss Baker, her phone reminded her.

I'm busy, she texted back.

Miss Baker!

Crap! She and Dad stood at the hub of mayhem, thankfully in the only decent shade from the brutal mid-day sun. The Pathfinder space shuttle—complete with the big orange tank and the two-side boosters—was the only full shuttle stack assembled anywhere. It anchored this end of the US Space and Rocket Center and cast a big shadow.

Today it also anchored HERC, the Human Exploration Rover Challenge. Two-person human-powered rovers were being prepared for an obstacle course by twenty-three high school and university teams. Dad was one of the official judges—along with a bunch of NASA scientists and astronauts. She was his assistant.

Miss Baker! The reminder echoed.

"Daddy, I've got to go see about something."

Senator Jerome Walker gave her one of those looks he wielded on the floor of the US Senate like a missile punching through sun-softened butter. "Pee fast and get back here. This is your campaign stop, not mine."

Kimberlee figured that assumption was easier than explaining anonymous messages and sprinted away. Besides, she needed to get away from the chief of NASA's Astronaut Office who'd just asked why she hadn't submitted an application.

She'd decided to follow her father into politics. It made

more sense, didn't it? From the government, she could fight to keep NASA funded. She couldn't do that from space.

All of the doubts were sending her stumbling about like her guidance system was on the fritz during liftoff. Hopefully no one was about to punch her abort-destruct button.

She raced around the corner of the main Space Camp building, the closest bathrooms, then hid and peeked back.

Even the campaign newsies hadn't followed her once they saw where she was headed. Dad's next reelection wasn't for two years. Her first election was in a couple months and she was doing well in the polls.

Mama had said start small, councilwoman for Huntsville. Deciding that she didn't have time to start small, Kimberlee was running for a vacated seat in the Alabama House of Representatives—she was still three years too young to be a senator. After kicking serious behinds in the primary, November was her focus, and the Rover Challenge was a campaign stop.

But the text message had been strange enough to get her attention.

Actually, it had been an excuse to get away from Senator Jerome Walker *and* NASA's chief astronaut, before they pulled her in two.

Ducking out through the security gate, with a wave for a guard she recognized but couldn't remember his name— she needed to work on that—she cut through the trees toward Miss Baker's grave.

It was a tall, slender gravestone for the first primate to survive a space flight. The small squirrel monkey and her companion Miss Able had rocketed up three hundred and sixty miles *and* survived the return. Up until then, the majority of test animals died in exploded rockets, failed reentries, or in capsules lost at sea. Able had died only days later during surgery to remove an infected electrode, but Miss Baker had become a national celebrity and gone on to become the longest-lived squirrel monkey on record by the time she died at twenty-seven.

Kimberlee was glad to see that there were a goodly number of bananas propped on the narrow top of the gravestone. Tourists often left them. Kimberlee herself had always made sure that a couple were in place before each Space Camp group's arrival tour.

A figure stood there with her back to Kimberlee, facing the tall gravestone. Even if Kimberlee hadn't recognized her, there was no doubting who it was, not with the brown-and-white Sheltie dog carefully inspecting the gravestone as well.

"Dilya!" Kimberlee threw herself into a welcoming hug. Dilya's natural reserve had never survived one of Kimberlee's onslaughts and crumbled this time as well. "God, haven't seen you in forever and nine-tenths more."

They'd gone to school on opposite coasts. Claremont McKenna had headhunted her straight out of the captaincy of their nationally ranked high school debate team. They'd only seen each other in person a few times over the last three years.

She held Dilya out at arm's length to inspect her for a moment, then dragged her back into a hug, which earned her one of Dilya's rare laughs.

"Hurry, tell me everything. No, better yet, come with me *and* tell me everything." Kimberlee tried to lead her away from the gravestone.

"Have you had any contact with Miss Watson?"

That stopped her in her tracks. Miss Watson wasn't the sort of person to be discussed around other people.

She noted the circles under Dilya's eyes, showing despite skin as medium-dark as her own, though a very distinct Uzbekistani hue rather than her own African American-Scottish-Italian mix. Her clothes were showing too many hours of travel and there was a dusty travel pack sitting on a nearby park bench.

"What happened?"

"She's gone."

"Where?"

Dilya used silence like a Saturn V rocket used a million pounds of thrust—it cut straight to the essentials.

"Well, ain't that a pickle now."

Dilya still didn't speak.

"Last time I had any contact was graduation. She sent me a small library of Presidential debates and commentaries—only not so small. Three of them were signed by the Presidents themselves...'to MW.' I'm guessing that's Miss Watson. I mean, I just can't believe she'd give me those."

"I never saw those in her library," Dilya squinted down at Zackie as if her dog knew. She gave a dog shake. Please let it be just a dog shake. The First Sheltie was smart, but not that smart, right?

"They're in mine now and I'm not giving them back. That's what convinced me to change tracks. I was headed," she pointed at the sky, "and now I'm running to be a state representative. Look, I have to get back. Come with me and we can talk tonight."

Dilya looked over her shoulder as if something urgent was calling her there. Her friend also looked exhausted in ways that had nothing to do with sleep.

She slung on Dilya's pack herself—which wasn't as heavy as it looked—grabbed her friend's hand and headed back without giving her any choice. Subject change. Dilya was fast, but subject changes at the speed a McKenna Debate Union captain could manage still threw her friend.

"How much do you know about space rovers?"

Dilya stumbled along in her wake and Zackie followed.

5

SHE SHOULD HAVE BEEN PAYING ATTENTION, BUT SHE'D NEVER been here and there was so much to see. Dilya gawked like any tourist who'd entered a park too close to closing. Everything was a blur, gone before she could really focus on it.

A distant cheer sounded as if there was a crowd somewhere.

By the front entrance, an A-12 Oxcart, the spy plane that had become the SR-71 Blackbird. The strange plane that looked as if it had been flattened until all that was left was a hundred and seven feet of blackness and sharp edges. It had flown above the Soviet Union at several times the speed of sound taking incredible photos.

Around the corner stood an entire Saturn V rocket resting on its tailfins. *Going to the moon? Hop on!* it beckoned.

The source of a round of groans were now visible. It wasn't a big crowd, but it was an involved one, close together in a winding line of some sort. Two lines, either side of a paved walkway.

That was the first place she was nearly run over.

A gangly contraption came racing at them from around the base of the rocket. Two people were aboard and pedaling fiercely. That sat back-to-back on a four-wheeled... thing that was half bicycle and half lunar rover. The wheels were mechanically articulated in strange ways that appeared to flex and bend as the rover passed by. There was almost nothing to it: four wheels, two axles flexing from a central shaft, and the two seats.

Kimberlee had stopped her in time to avoid bodily harm. The racecourse was marked off by yellow rope line strung along the tops of orange traffic cones. Strategic bales of hay had been placed at corners.

But this vehicle was in pain. Two of the flexy-wheels had flexed in ways that they couldn't recover from. But that didn't stop the two riders. Instead they fought it along the course as it veered and skittered through the lane as much sideways as forward.

"Go rovernauts! Go! Go! Go!" Kimberlee shouted encouragement as she dodged a particularly bad veer toward the ropes. Others lining the course added their shouts as heartily.

Once they were clear, Kimberlee glanced left but veered right, dodging through the back fringes of the crowd.

"I'm supposed to be over there, but you simply haveta see this. Look, it's a LEM Lunar Lander in the middle of a cratered field."

The LEM wasn't the quality of the one at the Smithsonian Air and Space Museum but it was meant to be a model. The one in DC had been slated to go to space.

And there were the next contestants, battling their rover in and out of the dirt craters. Kimberlee stopped at a good vantage point.

"Each school team builds their own machine from

scratch. Like they can buy the wheel hubs but have to design and manufacture their own wheels. Each rover must fold up to smaller than a five-foot cube. And you get the most points if it's less than a hundred and thirty pounds and you can unfold and assemble it in under thirty seconds. Then they have to survive fourteen obstacles. There are five sample-retrieval science tasks, too. Tough ones they had to design tools to beat."

From here Dilya could see several of them, each punctuated by a Kimberlee Kommentary, called Kay-Kays within the group. In high school, she was the one who always had a cool factoid or story about everything, from all of her debate club research.

A big hump to climb and descend had been built across the normal walkway that was now a racecourse. "A lot tougher than it looks. It's a matter of gearing to go fast on the flat but have a low enough gear to climb that."

A six-inch wide pipe sticking up from the ground to well over the rovernauts heads. "They have to retrieve two hundred mils of water out the top without getting out of their seats."

The narrow pit of head-sized boulders didn't need any explanation. Nor did the sloshy area of deep pea gravel.

A pit with ten small fountains. "See that winding path through them? A serious steering test as you can't touch any of the ice geysers."

"The moon has ice geysers?" Dilya's head felt like it was plowing through mud, super-thick, extra-icy mud.

"No. Duh! But Europa might. NASA is always looking to get new ideas from us kids. They hire the good ones, too, which is very cool. Okay, I can't stay away any longer. C'mon."

Then they were hying off in another direction.

Kimberlee led them through a cluster of historical rockets planted like oversized sunflowers, far too tall for how big around they measured. A rover came racing down the straightaway, slowed abruptly, then crawled along a curved ramp that threatened to tip the rovernauts over sideways as if they were rounding the brow of a hill.

Kimberlee skidded to a halt. She never moved slowly. "Hi, Daddy. You remember Dilya Stevens from the high school Chef's Club?"

He opened his mouth, clearly ready to say something quite different, and closed it again. Jerome Walker put on his best US Senator face and held out a hand.

"Hello again, Ms. Stevens. How are things at the White House?" proving there was nothing wrong with his memory.

"They're—" and that's when she heard it. The fast *snick-snick-snick* of cameras. News cameras always sounded different because they never shot a single image. Every shutter release took ten or more shots, so the best could be chosen later.

Snick-snick-snick as they cut out pieces of her soul. She'd learned outer poise before the camera from two successive First Ladies, yet inside she reviled them with a deep harbored hatred.

And today of all days?

Doing a crap job of disappearing, Dilya. She could almost hear Miss Watson laughing that she'd walked into such a trap.

Too busy looking elsewhere, child. Keep your eyes and wits open.

Time to make the best of the situation.

"They're fine, Senator Walker. The First Lady has decided to give Zackie's puppies to each of the White House children. You can't imagine how happy that makes them."

The Senator offered her another of his smiles, recognizing a good sound bite when he heard one. "Oh, I can, Ms. Stevens. I've had the good fortune to own a couple of fine animals myself. Spaniels, good hunting and retrieving stock. Can't imagine a Sheltie hunts much?"

Pricked at the challenge, she almost stated that Zackie had been trained to be expert at tracking people and helping her track information. She caught herself in time and put on her best smile to match the Senator's. She pulled Kimberlee into the shot.

"You know, Kimberlee. Zackie is an absolute expert at..."

Kimberlee laughed at the memory, "...at hunting treats and naps." It's what everyone who didn't know better thought of Zackie. Other than a few dog trainers and her friends, that's what everyone thought.

Snick-snick-snick. It was a good moment. Highly photogenic. And Dilya had managed to tug Kimberlee into a primary blocking position. With her own hair shaken forward enough to mask her eyes to that side, little would show except her own smile.

Attention turned back to the rover challenge in stages.

First the others who'd been listening in, then the reporters, and finally the Senator until once again it was only herself and Kimberlee.

"What's going on?"

Kimberlee tapped the button pinned above her left breast: *Walker for Rep.*

"So?"

"I'm campaigning. Expand that to *Kimberlee Walker for Alabama Representative* and you'd be getting a might warmer. Also it's my motto, *For Real Representation.* I'm gonna ride the youth vote straight into office."

6

THE GEARS GROUND IN DILYA'S HEAD. IT WAS ONE TOO MANY changes in the same day.

Miss Watson gone.

Out of a job and, she only realized belatedly, a place to live. There was always Mom and Dad's, but the White House had been her home for almost every night of eight years.

Rootless. Not as rootless as she'd been while starving and freezing high in the Hindu Kush, but not anchored either.

Now Kimberlee, whose help she needed, stood solidly poised on her life's next step. Thinking back, Kimberlee had said she was running, but it had seemed more whimsical than real. Dilya knew she was going to be an astronaut. Everybody knew that.

But there *had* been that conversation.

State senate worked out for Obama.

Dilya had agreed and they'd talked about the steps he'd taken, and which would and wouldn't work for Kimberlee.

But they'd still been college juniors at the time, and it all felt academic. Not so much.

Dilya managed to stay in the background. Only one reporter had been on the ball enough to try for a follow-up interview with her. She was too old a hand to reveal anything important yet gave the impression that the reporter alone in the whole world had her exclusive view of life at the White House.

Give them the social tidbits and only the best will notice that you never said anything. Again, Miss Watson was right.

Rover after rover left and returned. Most made it to the finish within the eight-minute time limit. Those who couldn't were sent on, but required to use the bypass route at each remaining obstacle and received no more points.

Yet without fail, each who crossed the line—even the two who were towing their rover by the front axle with the broken front wheels in the passenger seats—were welcomed to the finish as heroes. They might collapse from the strain of the run, but not until they crossed the finish.

Each and every time, she was reminded of Miss Watson's instruction.

Think in teams, not individuals. It is my one great failing, don't let it be yours.

Dilya watched Kimberlee helping a team across the line who'd clearly suffered a bad rollover out on the course. They were scraped and bloody, an angry rash on one's arm and the other with a bad limp. But they were smiling.

As were the photographers who were following with their big lenses.

Dilya needed to build a team.

Kimberlee cheered up the battered team exactly as she always had for their circle all of the way back in high school.

Or did Dilya already have a team?

"No message or anything?" Kimberlee dropped some peanuts into her Dr. Pepper and listened to the merry fizz inside the can. The glass case surrounding the Apollo 16 capsule felt cool against her back after the long day in the sun.

The park had emptied with the end of the competition. Tomorrow they'd be back for award ceremonies and a big party. For now, she and Dilya had retreated into the closed Saturn V Museum while the groundskeepers disassembled the course. The vast hall, normally filled with hundreds, echoed with only the two of them and a dog, parking their butts on the floor at the farthest end.

Dilya chose to eat her peanuts rather than drink them. "Nothing. There four days ago, then gone as if she'd never been."

"Can't you ask—"

"*Who?*" Dilya voice rose in frustration. It sounded like a slap in the cavernous Saturn V Hall. The rocket had reigned as the tallest and most powerful ever built for over fifty years. This one was made of test modules and mockups.

Parts hung from the ceiling with the big first and second stages resting in steel cradles, all in a line—longer than a football field, end zones too.

Kimberlee really hadn't had that much to do with Miss Watson. Or didn't think she had. Instead it was...

"Hey!"

"What?" Dilya tossed a couple peanuts to Zackie who caught them in the air. She made a whole spectacle of crunching and chewing each nut that was fun to watch.

"All that stuff you said to me."

"What stuff?"

"Like when I was choosing colleges and courses. You always had all this advice. Was that you or her?"

Dilya stared a little too fixedly at the Lunar Excursion Module for landing on the Moon. This was a good model, far better than the mockup at the center of the lunar crater pit outside.

"Dil-ya..."

"It was good advice, wasn't it?"

"Yeah, but you're avoiding the question."

Dilya shook her head. "I honestly don't know. She can plant an idea in your head without you even knowing it. Like the *Inception* movie only for real. She was so stealth— and I miss her so much."

Her Dr. Pepper forgotten, Dilya pulled her legs up to her chest and buried her face against her knees. Zackie curled up on the toes of Dilya's shoes.

Kimberlee pulled her into a hug but didn't know what else to do. Seeing Dilya go fetal was a new one. Curled up tighter than an armadillo.

Dilya had always been the strong one.

The Chef's Club had been a cockamamie idea Valentina had cooked up, almost literally. The tall, blonde valedictorian was the *perfect girl* of high school, complete with the lovely accent inherited from her mother and father, the Defense Attaché at the French Embassy in DC. Tired of all of the peer-believing worship from the girls who had clustered about her, Valentina had struck out in a new direction.

She recruited three others as uncomfortable with in-the-box thinkers as herself. Then she'd come up with an out-of-the-box idea to make them think differently. Every month they'd reached out to a new restaurant and asked to spend a weekend shadowing the kitchen chefs. Even Trevor, the only one of them who could really cook was amazed at what they learned. It wasn't only food; it was class and culture and personal histories of places they couldn't have found in DC. But they did.

The Chef's Club. The secret society of dissatisfied misfits.

Until they'd talked their way into the White House kitchen and met Dilya. A Uzbekistani war orphan, adopted by a Special Operations Forces helicopter team. A resident of the White House itself, who traveled all over the world with the First Family, with successive First Families. She was even the protégé of a secret spy hidden in the basement, which was beyond cool.

They'd inducted her that weekend and formed a new clique at school.

Kimberlee held Dilya tighter.

Valentina had remained the leader, she herself was the voice. Trevor was the steadfast one and Jimmy the nerd. But Dilya had been their strength. They'd gathered together in the lunchroom and the outings to various restaurant kitchens. But over the years they'd spent far more time discussing, debating, and breaking down any idea that came to hand.

Kimberlee still missed it. Five high school kids convinced they could fix the world if they just thought about it hard enough. Politics, food supply, energy distribution, one of Trevor's recipes. It didn't matter what, they chased it.

Dilya had begun slipping some of their ideas into the Oval Office, much as Kimberlee had slid a few into her own father's ear. Senator Jerome Walker had proposed more than one bill with Chef's Club ideas in it, brought up over dinner and dropped into a conversation.

But Miss Watson?

How was she supposed to help Dilya find Miss Watson? Leave her campaign? The numbers said that she was polling solidly—*very* solidly, though she was keeping her hopes in check.

Her hopes.

How had Miss Watson known to give her a complete library of Presidential debates? They'd become her recreational reading. Recreational? Ha! She'd consumed them, could quote whole passages of Lincoln-Douglas, Kennedy-Nixon, right up to the madness of more recent contests.

Somehow Miss Watson had known of her most secret desire, to sit behind the Roosevelt Desk in Oval Office as President one day.

That day of the interview. Four years ago and it still stood out as a shining moment in her life.

Dilya had convinced the President to let them ask him questions for a full thirty minutes, right there in the Oval. Whose idea had it been to let her sit in the chair? Had she asked? Was it Dilya or Miss Watson somehow suggesting to Dilya to set that up? That brief moment felt so real that, even sitting here on the hard floor with her back against the Apollo display case, she knew that was the reality she wanted.

Only because it had been a childhood dream could Kimberlee be sure that Miss Watson hadn't actually planted that idea in her head as well.

And once more she was back to the books Miss Watson had given her. She was a librarian. A librarian of the most comprehensive library of spy craft perhaps anywhere—she certainly had several pithy observations to make about the quality of the CIA's own, much larger library.

"Her library."

Dilya didn't respond.

Kimberlee shook her. Shook her hard enough that Zackie growled at her.

"Shush!" she said to the dog. "Snap out of it, Dilya," she said to her friend. "The library."

Only after she accidentally shook Dilya hard enough to bang her head on the glass and glare at her did Kimberlee stop.

"Think. Her library. Where did it go?"

"Gone. With her."

"Ding!" Kimberlee wanted to shout, but it was hard to shout such a silly word with appropriate sarcasm.

Dilya and her dog looked at her as if she'd lost her mind.

"With *her*. Did she ever *not* have a plan in place? Did she ever *not* know who was coming there to her office? Nobody could get that library out of there, except her. Even if they did, the teapot? The Snoopy dog biscuit jar? Where did that collection go?"

8

SLAPPING HER HANDS TO HER MOUTH DIDN'T MUFFLE THE YELP that shot from her mouth to echo down the entire length of the Saturn V rocket.

A moment ago, Dilya had lost her mother all over again. The ridiculously small sound of the Makarov PMM pistol that had punched such a small hole through father's and then mother's foreheads, ringing once more in her ears until it was the only sound in the world. Only in nightmares had she ever returned to that high mountain valley to watch the two men kill her parents.

It was weird, she didn't know the murderers' names. Her adoptive mother did, for she had killed them in turn to stop a war, but it wasn't the sort of thing she'd ever dared ask about. It was a closed chapter best left behind them.

But Kimberlee was right, and she'd never seen it.

"So, she's out there still, somewhere," Kimberlee sounded as confident about that as she did about almost everything. No wonder she was polling so high, she spoke honesty from the heart.

"In trouble," Dilya began piecing it together. "But out of

the White House by her own choice. But why leave no clue for me?"

"Maybe she knew they were coming for her and didn't want to chance it. Maybe because she knew you'd figure it out on your own."

Dilya looked at her friend, "But I didn't. You did."

"Hey, what are friends for?"

Sun Tzu's maxim, 'Keep your friends close and your enemies closer.' A haughty Miss Watson sniff of disdain. *Utter hogwash, child. Nothing is more powerful than a group of friends working toward a common goal.*

9

DILYA WAS GONE WHEN KIMBERLEE AWOKE.

They'd talked most of the night. Some of it about old times, some of it about their friends from Chef's Club and where they were now. A lot about Kimberlee's possible routes to national office.

Kimberlee had remembered that she'd once seen Trevor having tea, no one drank anything else around Miss Watson, with her. It had been in a small cafe-bookstore close by the Hay-Adams Hotel where his mother was head chef.

It had been late when she'd tossed off the memory, thinking nothing more of it.

Not until Kimberlee found the note tucked inside her pajama pocket.

Off for some T. I'll vote for you. D.

Kimberlee rubbed her thumb across the note. It was silly, but she could feel Dilya there in the letters.

She was going to find Trevor and discuss his teatime with Miss Watson. Off to gather the next piece of the chain to lead her to Miss Watson.

Then Kimberlee read the note once more and began to laugh.

Dilya was a legal resident of Washington, DC. She couldn't vote for Kimberlee to enter the Alabama House any more than she could for the US Senate.

But she could certainly vote for her as President.

"Well," Kimberlee tucked the note away where she'd never lose it, "that's one vote. Only eighty million or so to go."

Her course now lay clear before her. She wondered how long until Dilya's did.

PART TWO

THE LIBRARY TRAIL

1

"Not so normal, huh, Zackie?"

In reply, the Sheltie gave her a sad look from inside her carrier. Neither of them were used to traveling this way.

For Dilya's first nine years, travel had been on foot or in the back of a dusty farm truck with tools, animals, or produce during harvest season. All part of being poor in Uzbekistan. But it was okay there, because everyone she'd ever known was poor. It was their normal state.

Three years of traveling with the American military as an adopted war orphan meant she'd never had to think about where she was going or how she'd get there.

Then from twelve to nineteen—as the First Nanny and later also the First Dog Sitter—she'd gone where the President had gone. More importantly, she'd gone the *way* the President had gone: Marine One, the Presidential motorcade, and Air Force One.

Dilya and former First Dog Zackie were now cut loose from the whole apparatus. Four days ago she'd flown from Washington to the First Family's farm in Tennessee aboard Air Force One—then simply left. A crisis had arisen and she had no choice. Rather than trying to stop her, the First Lady had given Zackie to Dilya and sent them away with her best wishes.

Together, she and the former First Dog were rapidly discovering aspects of American culture she'd never imagined—like how big it was from a train car.

"I'll get you out soon," she hated lying to her dog. They'd traveled from Tennessee down to Huntsville, Alabama to ask for help from a friend. That hadn't been so bad. From Alabama to Washington, DC, was twenty hours of horrible. Next time she didn't care what it cost, she wasn't going coach. With a sleeping compartment, at least she could let Zackie out of the carrier.

"We need a car." She'd never thought about that much —transportation had come with the job. And living in the heart of DC had made a car redundant—though she was a good driver. Training didn't get any better than Reese Carver, the lead driver of the The Beast, the President's limousine. In high school, Reese had even helped her finagle training for all of her Chef's Club out at the Secret Service's James J. Rowley Training Center.

The Chef's Club. Maybe they could help her.

It originally had four members, she was the fifth. *They* had all been clique leaders in high school: debate, athlete, social, and nerd. But they'd grown tired of those narrow views and formed a new social group—their own.

As part of breaking out of their norms, they'd added Dilya for reasons that still bewildered her. Working and living at the White House since Junior High, she'd been the ultimate misfit in high school even by DC standards. Yet for the last two years of school, the five members of the Chef's Club had become inseparable. At least until college had sent them off in a dozen directions—well, four actually. She had remained in DC and attended Georgetown in between her responsibilities at the White House.

Zackie whined at her from her carrier.

"Right. That does it." Dilya had memorized the train stops out of habit—she'd been taught to always be prepared —and she knew the next big town was less than ten minutes away. Seven minutes on her phone and she had her model ordered from existing stock at the dealership.

Two hours later, she and Zackie slid into their new British racing-green Hybrid MINI Cooper and were once more on the road to DC. There were definite advantages to having all of her expenses paid by the government on top of the salary that the First and Second families had paid her for the last eight years. She'd never spent a dollar she didn't have to. And saved every penny.

And she'd looked up the law. Living in the White House and overhearing all that she did, haddn't *quite* earmarked her investment strategy as insider trading. It was a public building after all.

2

Trevor Nolan had done it.

Sort of.

He'd spent his high school summers, when he wasn't at soccer practice, working in this kitchen. During those summers, he'd slowly risen from dishwasher to *mise en place*. For the months between junior and senior year, he and three others had entered the Hay-Adams Hotel's kitchen while DC was still dark. Together they'd prepared all of the ingredients needed for the day. A slow path from washing vegetables, through grinding spices, to actually cutting the vegetables and cleaning the fish—though none of them were ever allowed to actually cut the fish into portions.

Mother might be demanding, driven, and a borderline psychotic, but she was also the head chef at The Lafayette inside the Hay-Adams Hotel. A Michelin star might continue to allude her, but there was no beating her address —directly across Lafayette Square from the White House.

It was also the only time in his life he ever saw her. He didn't know why he'd kept coming here, Dad had left long ago. A DC cop, he'd long since remarried and they'd made a great home for Trevor in the process. Yet the kitchen drew him back into his Mom's sphere time after time.

Last month, after three years training in Paris, Trevor had only intended to come home for a week or so while he'd sorted out where he wanted to go next. After nailing Le Cordon Bleu's *Grand Diplôme de Cuisine et Pâtisserie* course, he'd worked as a kitchen slave in three Parisian two-star restaurants for six months each. Three years abroad was enough. It was time to climb out of the dungeon; he wanted to work somewhere better than troll level.

New York. He'd planned on heading to New York after catching up with some of his old soccer mates in DC. Except Mom's grillardin had broken his leg while waterskiing on Chesapeake Bay that first weekend after Trevor's return.

And he had thought the French were tough to work for. He'd never cooked on the line for Mom before and now knew better.

"Three dover sole, two filet, and an Amish chicken," she called out the last as if it was beneath her—probably because it was her sous chef's recipe. Still, a three-hundred-and-fifty-dollar order from the grill alone didn't strike him as scoff-worthy. He already had three orders down and wouldn't have enough open burners for another thirty seconds. Not if he wanted to get the timing right so that everything finished at the same moment, permitting clean service to the table.

Sure enough, at twenty-three seconds, Chef Mom swung by his station. "The order isn't down yet? Jesus, Trevor. Get it together."

"Yes, chef!" He hadn't called her Mom since his sixth birthday, which she hadn't attended but instead sent a chef to make hazelnut crème brûlées for all his six-year-old buddies who wanted chocolate cake with a major load of icing.

His response went unheard as she'd already moved on to harangue Margo over the state of her black truffle crab gnocchi orders at the next station.

His phone buzzed as he began plating the prior orders. He was too well trained to let it break his rhythm and he emptied pan after pan onto a wide variety of stoneware. As soon as the expediter grabbed them he queued up the next set of plates under the warmer.

No meal at the Lafayette would ever be left to cool and fade past perfect under the infrared lights, they were only for pre-warming the plates.

He risked a glance at the text message.

Horse butt.

From an unlisted number but that didn't mater. It had been three years since he'd last seen that same message, but only one person could have sent it.

Trevor failed to cover his laugh.

His mother, attracted by his reaction like a food critic to a lone fish scale on their plate, snapped at him, "You have no pans down."

The expediter had already whisked away all other evidence of his work.

"I don't know why I ever bothered having you, Trevor. You're a waste of space." She nodded toward the stack of empty sauté pans. "Get your ass in gear. No special dispensation for being my son or having some fancy diploma from Cordon Bleu. Not in my kitchen."

Horse butt, his phone automatically refreshed the message.

"Yes chef." He intended to reach for the pans he needed, he really did.

But his hand snagged the tie on his apron as he stuffed his phone into his back pocket.

As if his hand had a mind of its own, it didn't stop there. Once it had begun untying his apron, it finished the job. He folded it neatly, watching his hands with some surprise, as they set it on the work ledge along the front of the grill.

Chef-Mom's glare heated up faster than an empty copper Mauviel pan.

He doffed his immaculate white chef's jacket. Folding it neatly as well, he rested it atop his apron.

"You can't leave in the middle of service, Trevor Nolan. Now you just—"

He pulled out his phone again, now that his hands were once more under his control, and tapped the screen awake to see the message.

"I should have done this long ago."

Then Trevor turned it to face his Mom.

Horse butt.

3

"I DON'T KNOW WHAT CAME OVER ME."

Dilya didn't speak, of course—she didn't very often. But she'd met the former Mrs. Nolan, which saved Trevor a lot of explaining. The current one, Trevor's stepmom, was light-years nicer. DC cop tough, had to be to keep up with Dad, but awesome anyway. He needed to remember to tell her that more often than he already did.

"And, yeah, I really did show her your message with no explanation. I then grabbed a packet of tartare-grade Kobe beef and walked out."

Zackie was happily working her way through the treat.

"That's probably a hundred-dollar snack for the First Dog. Guess that's my severance pay." And the chances of Mom ever speaking to him again were probably worse than none. He couldn't decide how he felt about that. Relieved or plain old sad? A strife-ridden segment of his life now had the door firmly slammed in its face. But knowing his Mom was a cast-iron bitch and accepting it were too different challenges.

Horse butt.

Dilya and Zackie had been sitting in their normal meeting spot, on the lawn of Lafayette Park directly opposite the horse butt of Andrew Jackson's statue. It placed the North Portico of the White House to their left and the Hay-Adams to the right.

Tourists were drawn like magnets to the south edge of the park to photograph the White House. Locals crisscrossed the park with determined strides, iced coffees, and a minimum of chatter. It was a great place to sit on the lawn—often they were the only ones in the whole park not on the move—and talk as anonymously as if they were in a secret chamber. Today their spot was near perfect. The first days of September had abated the summer's heat but still promised many more, glorious beneath the arch of the blue sky. The white marble buildings of DC appeared etched against it like the finest sugar lacework on a black forest gateau.

The two of them had used the park a lot during high school because it was so convenient for both of them.

"I guess this is a bit less convenient now that I've burned the bridge with Mom." *Oh. My. God?* Or *About freaking time?* Nope, he still had no idea which.

"Is it okay if I say about time, Trevor?" Dilya's voice was as soft as she looked. Long ruffly brown hair, darkish skin, and vibrant green eyes that saw everything.

"Yeah, I guess." After all, Dilya was the smartest one in a group of overachievers, so she was probably right.

"My adoptive family are the ones I call Mom and Dad. My mother and father were shot dead when I was nine." Which reminded him that Dilya might *look* soft, but was pure steel inside.

"Really? Sorry, I didn't know." How could he not know that about her?

"I never talk about it."

"Dilya, you hardly talk at all. But when you do, it's always so damn interesting."

She didn't respond as a trio of flash teenagers eased by in crop tops and Lycra shorts so short that even the DC midday heat didn't justify them. Not that he was complaining about the view.

"Zackie isn't First Dog anymore," she said it so softly that he almost lost it under the trio's inane chatter about some band he'd never heard of. He was only twenty-one, for crying out loud, what was up with that?

"I don't think that's the kind of position you can get unelected from. Maybe an act of Congress, but that seems rather extreme especially for the current group of lunatics under the Capitol Dome who can't agree on a lunch order. What did you do, Zackie?" At being addressed, the Sheltie rolled onto her back asking for a belly rub. He gave her one.

"The First Lady gave her to me when I quit my job."

"She gave you— Wait! Like quit the White House?" Dilya was such a fixture there it was hard to imagine the building without her. "Got sick of it after, what, your *third* administration? President Matthews once and two terms for President Zachary Thomas, right?"

"No. I loved it." She was staring very fixedly at the horse's butt. So much so that Trevor finally understood what she was actually doing was very carefully *not* looking at the White House.

"When was this?"

"Three days ago."

"Holy crap, Dilya. And you've been letting me ramble on with a blow-by-blow of Mom's insanity? Are you okay with it?" All he'd done was call his own mother a horse's butt in her own kitchen and walk out. Dilya had been kicked out of the *White House*.

"I don't know. I don't think I'm okay. But I didn't have a lot of choice."

"You didn't have any choice about quitting? The President threw you out but gave you his dog?"

"No, I quit on my own. And it was the First Lady who let me keep Zackie." Dilya had taken over the belly rub once Trevor stopped.

Zackie appeared to both hum with pleasure and fall asleep at the same time with all four paws in the air and her head laid back upon the grass.

"Why did you quit?"

Dilya finally looked away from the horse's butt and turned to face him for the first time. "Tell me what you know about Miss Watson."

"She's your friend, or mentor, or whatever." The Chef's Club had met with her once in the deepest basement in the White House. The old woman was an ex-spymaster who maintained a library of spy craft. She had served their group fine tea and homemade butter cookies in an unlikely elegant sitting room behind the battered steel door of Mechanical Room 043. Dilya had been her protégé as far as anyone in the Chef's Club could guess. The next great female spymaster? Jimmy had tried labeling her the NGFSM but it hadn't stuck.

"I need to know what *you* know." Dilya's typical mood rarely emerged from completely serious but never before with this heavy directness.

"Is this some kind of test? You said we weren't supposed to talk about her."

"No, Trevor, it's not a test. She's gone missing. I had to

leave the White House to try and figure out what happened to her."

"Gone missing? Like, kidnapped?"

Dilya shrugged uncertainly before looking away to stare at the sleeping Zackie. "Her office is barren. Not empty, barren. She's gone. Her entire library is gone. The sitting room. All of it. Kimberlee said you once met her for tea here, above ground."

4

DILYA COULD FEEL THE CHANGE IN TREVOR'S INTEREST THE moment she mentioned Kimberlee. He'd had a huge crush on her in high school. If they'd ever actually gone out, she'd never seen any evidence of it. It was perhaps a little weird that the tall, handsome, soccer team captain—who could have any girl he wanted—had focused on the feisty, hyper-driven, debate-team-captain. The senator's daughter from Alabama.

Kimberlee appeared to have never noticed, which was impossible. But it was also Kimberlee who Dilya had met with in Huntsville two days ago and who had sent her to see Trevor about Miss Watson.

She'd known exactly where Trevor was. Which said what about the two of them?

Dilya hadn't even realized that he'd returned from Paris yet.

"The teas," Trevor didn't ask about Kimberlee. "I'd almost forgotten about them."

"Teas plural?"

"Sure. All through senior year. I'd get a note every

couple weeks to appear at one DC tea room or another. She said the exposure would do my palate good."

"What else did you talk about?" And how hadn't she known that one of her closest friends had meetings with her mentor?

"Soccer, especially the problems with American soccer. A lot of schools were scouting me pretty hot and heavy. A couple of the pro teams were too. But she pointed out that soccer was a tough sell in America. It doesn't get much airtime here in the States because there isn't enough time for ad breaks. TV networks tried to change the rules when the World Cup came here in 1994 to allow for more ad breaks. In American football, they can do micro ads between downs and ad breaks when teams change the field, during time outs, and a whole lot more. Pro and college soccer, with two forty-five minute halves and no real breaks in the action is a tough sell here."

"And Miss Watson knew about all that?" Because Dilya certainly hadn't. She saw a couple of people she knew from the White House come out the North Gate and start across Lafayette Park. She shifted her lean so that she was behind Trevor when their eyes might have glanced this way. Then they were gone. It was okay that she was here, but she didn't want to be distracted by idle greetings or have to explain why she was in DC with Zackie while the First Family was in Tennessee.

"Can you tell me something she didn't know about?" Trevor craned around to look at her. She sat upright once more.

Dilya had to admit that she'd never run into anything. But Miss Watson had only ever served two teas in her office: Murchie's #10 black tea before three in the afternoon and a fine decaf green mint tea afterward. Trevor was implying she was a tea aficionado. And she'd never once mentioned sports of any kind in Dilya's presence.

"Looking back, I guess those afternoon teas are probably what sent me down the path of chef rather than soccer. And not merely chef, but the Grand Diplôme at Le Cordon Bleu. Oh, and at each tea, she'd have the host give me a couple of dessert recipes, then quiz me about them at our next meeting. How many times had I made them? What would I change? How? Why?"

Dilya tried to see where this was leading but had no idea how it could help her find Miss Watson.

"Did she have a favorite?"

"Ching Ching CHA," Trevor spoke without hesitation. "It's over on Embassy Row in Georgetown."

Dilya had no idea what it meant or what her next step might be. At a loss, she looked at Trevor. "Want to go have some tea?"

5

_____

"Uh," Trevor looked at the slick little MINI Cooper. It was so new that it sparkled. Then he looked in through the windshield at the passenger seat. "I think there's a bit of a problem."

Dilya looked at him over the roof of the car. "Really? I bought the four-door version for a reason."

Trevor laughed. Did Dilya even think of it as rude? Probably not. Though Dilya didn't miss much, so maybe it was all her idea of an ironic joke. Zackie was definitely _people_ to her. She opened the driver door and Zackie bounded into the car, across the driver's seat, and landed in the passenger seat—where a plush dog bed was buckled into place. It had four high raised sides and a thick bottom that raised the Sheltie enough to stare at him through the window without having to stretch to see. Was Zackie smirking?

Well, that tells you where you rate, Trevor. He opened the back door and climbed in behind the dog.

He'd hardly been in a car since high school. There

wasn't a lot of use for them in Paris, especially not when working the kind of hours he'd been.

"They told me to take it easy until the motors are broken in." She punched a search into the nav system as she spoke. He could have told her how to get there but he wasn't fast enough for the speed of Dilya's thoughts.

"Motors? Plural?" That sounded like a good excuse to buckle up quickly.

"It's a hybrid. The electric motors on each wheel make it nice and punchy." Then without a sound, Dilya went from parked along Lafayette Park to whipping her way through DC afternoon traffic like a NASCAR driver.

That's when he remembered that they'd all been trained by a former NASCAR racer turned Presidential chauffeur— and Dilya had been the best of them.

She started with whipping a U-ie onto Pennsylvania Ave.

"Hang on, Zackie," he whispered as she whipped around five of the eight spokes of the Washington Circle rotary, and punched the gas out to M Street. Except the engine ran so quietly that it must still be in electric mode. She punched the volts? Amps? He was a chef and had no idea.

Zackie sat in her plush front seat throne with her head happily stuck out the window. He was glad to see that Dilya had snapped a leash to her collar. On Wisconsin, she chucked another sharp U-ie and pulled up alongside a tiny parking spot. She took her hands off the wheel and the car backed itself in as neatly as could be.

"I'm still alive, right?"

Dilya laughed, she actually laughed. "You never did really get the hang of DC driving, did you?"

"Not like that."

6

SHE'D NEVER BEEN TO CHING CHING CHA, HADN'T EVER heard of it. Dilya found that seriously disturbing. A piece of Miss Watson's past...well, she'd had decades and decades of a past before Dilya was born. But to have this piece of *recent* past elude her felt as if she stood on a sinking dinghy.

Every minute that she slowed down, Miss Watson slipped one step further away. How could she help a person she couldn't catch up to? Worse, a person she knew so much less about than she'd thought.

Miss Watson had given Kimberlee her personal collection of Presidential debates, going all the way back to the Lincoln-Douglas debates—the Senatorial race that Abraham Lincoln had lost. The gift had inspired her to enter politics rather than apply to be an astronaut.

Kimberlee had also given Dilya the clue to try and follow the library to find the person. Miss Watson had known something and managed to smuggle her spy-craft library out of the White House without anyone the wiser—including Dilya.

Trevor, on the other hand, had been led to tea houses to

train his palate and orient his thinking toward a different future, despite the soccer scholarships schools had offered him. Dilya couldn't see how this was relevant to anything.

Ching Ching CHA was about the least impressive storefront Dilya had ever seen. It had a narrow front among a long line of businesses crowded against the Chesapeake and Ohio Canal—which had never reached the Ohio River even in its heyday, now a century gone.

The dark wood fronting looked old and in need of a good sanding and varnish. *Ching Ching CHA – a Chinese tea house* may have once been painted in gold where it was carved into a black signboard above the door. It commanded a bare four yards along the shaded brick sidewalk. The bright flowers, curbside tables, and ridiculous statuary of the next door Italian restaurant only added to the shabby impression.

"Seriously, Trevor?"

He nodded and held the door for her.

A dim corridor led deeper into the building, which opened up into such a glorious space that Dilya couldn't catch her breath.

Two stories above, massive skylights let the daylight shine in. It shone down on white painted walls, dark-wood-trimmed arches, and little tables for four surrounded by elegant chairs in the same rich varnish as the grand arches. There was a raised platform area with low tables for having tea at floor level. A small kitchen filled the air with rich scents and rows of earthen jars painted a deep red were lined up on shelves.

Amid the rustle of soft voices and easy laughter, a small Chinese matron, perhaps as old as Miss Watson, threaded her way from one table to the next. At one she placed a black-iron teapot on a small burner. At another she gathered up stray dishes. Her twin, except for being half as old, delivered bento boxes from a tiny kitchen in the corner.

"Miss Watson always called this her tea library."

Dilya jolted so abruptly that Zackie whined a question.

"*Fan,*" she gave the Scottish Gaelic command for *wait*. Most war dogs were trained in German but Shelties were from the Shetlands: small, tough, sheep herders. Actually, Zackie was trilingual, English for the basic commands from the First Family, German from the many hours she'd spent hanging out with other Secret Service dogs, and Gaelic as their own private language.

"Fan of what?"

Dilya shook her head to silence Trevor.

Miss Watson's tea *library*. That was the key word. Miss Watson had *died* years before, at least she said she had as far as the CIA knew. She'd originally introduced herself to Dilya not as a former spy but rather as the leading librarian of spy craft in the US, which probably meant in the world.

"C'mon," Trevor led her to one of the tables on the raised wooden platform. "We always sat here for our tea." They took off their shoes, climbed the two steps, and sat at the low table.

"Is this where Miss Watson always sat?"

"On the same floor pillow where your butt is parked, Dilya." Trevor sat down across from her in an awkward cross-leg. At a hand signal, Zackie curled up between her and the back platform close by the back wall, mostly out of sight. No one had complained when she'd arrived with a dog, though Zackie was the only one here.

The older lady had walked over, shed her lime-green Crocs at the steps, and was now frozen in place holding the steaming teapot inches above the burner. She looked at both of them carefully before setting the teapot the rest of the way down over the low flame.

Trevor may not have noticed the hesitation, but the woman had Dilya's full attention.

"Welcome back to DC, Mr. Trevor." The woman gave a small bow.

"You remember me? I've been out of the States for the three years since I was last here with Miss Watson."

"One does not wisely forget a guest of the woman you mentioned. Please do not do so again." She bowed once more and was gone before Dilya could stop her.

"Well, that was weird."

No, Trevor had definitely used the wrong descriptor.

7

_____

WAS IT CHANCE OR PLANNING THAT KEPT THE OLD WOMAN from returning to their table? Dilya spotted no obvious intent to avoid.

Instead, it was the younger one who took their order. There were starters or a *Tea Meal,* with three choices. Trevor took the Mustard Miso Salmon and she ordered the Mapo Tofu. The bento boxes were delivered with a generous scoop of perfect white rice, three tastings of cooked vegetables, and a healthy serving of the entrée.

The green tea was good, as fine as any she'd had at the White House.

At the server's polite inquiry, Dilya assured the woman that Zackie had recently eaten, but a bowl of water would be appreciated.

As subtly as she could, Dilya checked the underside of the table for hidden messages—nothing—while quizzing Trevor.

"All we ever talked about was cooking. She was polite about it, but was never interested in soccer. Dad didn't like me following in Mom's footsteps, but my stepmom was big on following my passion. Is that what Kimberlee said she was doing? I was so sure she was headed to outer space."

Dilya wished he'd stay focused, but maybe he was...for his *own* thoughts and questions. "There's a legacy of both in her family. Her father and grandfather worked at Marshall Space Flight Center, before her dad become a US Senator. I think she was torn between the two, but Miss Watson helped her figure out that she was more interested in a lifetime in DC than decades of training for a few months in space."

"That...woman," he stumbled over not using Miss Watson's name, "was wild. What did she do to you?"

Dilya hadn't ever thought of it that way. She'd simply been Miss Watson—the spy turned librarian in the White House subbasement. Her friend.

Zackie woke up long enough to study her intently. Maybe even mentioning her, though not by name, had been enough to turn the Sheltie from dreams of dog biscuits to wishing she had real ones.

"I honestly don't think she did anything *to* me. She just..."

"Taught you shit that no one else on the planet could possibly know or understand."

Dilya closed her eyes. Again, even with this good friend, she was *other*. The outsider. The strange girl who lived in the White House and now hunted her lost teacher.

"She taught you?" A woman's voice.

Dilya opened her eyes to see the older server kneeling on a pillow at their table as she gathered up their empty bento boxes.

"This is her protégé," Trevor announced proudly.

"Trevor! Shush!" As if such things were acceptable public knowledge. He'd always been a little bit of a bull in a

China shop. Which was especially appropriate at the moment, bull in the Chinese tea shop.

"Ah!" the matron said on a soft breath. "The girl from White House. She said to watch for you."

Again Dilya twitched to focus on the woman, waking Zackie halfway back to her nap. She didn't like revealing her emotions so obviously.

"When? When did she say that? How recently?" Maybe this was finally the clue she'd been hunting.

"Oh, three maybe four—"

Dilya's hopes soared. Miss Watson had gone missing five to eight days ago.

"—year past."

The blow landed so hard in her gut that the Mapo Tofu barely stayed down. "Nothing more recent? When did you last hear from her?"

The elderly Chinese woman narrowed her eyes as she concentrated until all that remained were the wrinkles. "Two month ago. She have Kung Pao chicken."

"Do you know where she's gone?"

"Gone?" The woman stacked the bento boxes, then topped off their cups with the teapot.

"She left. Approximately a week ago. No note. Gone."

"She be back," the woman pushed to her feet.

"No. Her library is gone too."

This time the woman stared at her hard. "You have seen her library?"

"Many times."

"Whoosh, even Suyuan never see her library."

"Who's that?"

The woman smiled for the first time and tapped her own chest. "That is me. Number One tea librarian. You sure library is gone?"

Dilya nodded.

"No sign?"

Dilya reached out a hand to stroke Zackie. "None."

The woman turned her intent gaze on the Sheltie, then once more on Dilya. "Both more than they appear, yet she elude you both. This is very not good."

"I didn't need to hear that out loud." Dilya had kept hoping that the fear was only her own imaginings. Perhaps Miss Watson had finally retired in full. Perhaps even now there was a postcard from a French beach—though Miss Watson hadn't been a big fan of the French—awaiting her at the White House. Those pipe dreams evaporated like the smoke they were.

Suyuan tipped her head toward Trevor without turning to him. "This one. He can keep mouth shut?"

"When he has to."

8

—————

"WHAT ARE WE DOING HERE? WE HAD LUNCH LIKE HALF AN hour ago."

Dilya didn't explain herself as she led him toward the back door.

Pauley's Island had received two Michelin stars while he was overseas in Paris. Dilya was the one who'd arranged a kitchen tour and cooking lesson here for the Chef's Club. She'd pulled it off because one of her Night Stalkers secret helicopter regiment friends was the eldest son of the family. The Maloneys had created a whole in-the-know DC trend of Caribbean food. Getting a table here was beyond ridiculous, yet Dilya walked in the back door as if she was family.

Trevor adored this kitchen. Spacious, immaculately clean, with a big family dining table as a fixture. It was early afternoon and much of the family was seated there, eating their own lunch before prep started for dinner service. No knives striking cutting board, frying sizzles, or even a running dishwasher. For this brief moment the kitchen was all potential, no action. Except for the people.

The whirlwind of fluid Spanglish—the language of any

high-end kitchen in America, but doubly so at Pauley's—that washed around the table, didn't break when he and Dilya entered. Instead it swelled to include them.

Protests of a recent meal were ignored, and soon they were squeezed in with the others with generous portions mounded on plates before them. Zackie didn't appear the least bit hesitant about two meals in a row.

Trevor tasted more than he ate, but the flavors were magnificent, especially for a staff meal. There were spices here he knew nothing about. The smoothness of fresh papaya paired with roasted Doctor and Wrenchman fish and the least addition of garlic, pepper...

"White pepper? And..."

"Yes, and dried pimento," someone answered. It was amazing.

News flowed back and forth.

Nothing about Miss Watson, of course. Their only connection would be Dilya.

But he was soon being questioned about his coursework at Le Cordon Bleu and the restaurants he'd worked in since.

Eventually most of them had returned to prep the dinner service but Cara and Jackson. The elderly couple who had founded Pauley's as chef and manager, remained at the table with him. They were easy to talk to. And while they cared as passionately about the food as Mother or any of the French restaurants he'd slaved in, they also cared about their people.

Dilya, who had kept quiet except when directly questioned, finally spoke up to the Maloneys for the first time. "You'll have to be really obvious. Trevor is a little slow about certain things."

"I am not."

She rolled her eyes at him. "Kimberlee?"

Okay. That was valid. He didn't know how he'd let her slip away after high school. *In* high school. They'd never... and he still didn't know why.

"Did you know that she's set her sights on the White House? She's too young for the US House of Representatives, so she's getting elected in Alabama first. But I'll owe you a steak dinner if she isn't here in four years. And you know she's going to make every excuse to be at her father's side in the US Senate to make connections during that time."

Kimberlee living in Washington, DC? Coming back here?

Cara was smiling at him.

"Oh," Jackson sat up abruptly then his smile matched his wife's.

"What? I'm going to be in New York. I figure that's a good place to—"

"Can't say as you are, young man!" Jackson shook his head.

"What?"

"This is far better, Trevor. I did mention that small cottage in the Bahamas that we see too little of?"

Trevor looked at the older couple smiling at him.

"Six months," Cara said. "Three if he's as good as I think he is. Oh, Jackson, after all these years take more time off there by Christmas."

Trevor opened his mouth, then closed it.

This was a kitchen run like a family. No, it was a family that merely happened to run a two-star Michelin kitchen. And he'd just been invited in.

And Kimberlee was headed to DC.

No handshake was needed. No words. He simply took

another forkful of the fish, waved it at Cara, then closed his eyes to savor the masterful balance of flavors on his tongue.

If this worked, he'd be assisting...or possibly *running* the kitchen by Christmas? And Pauley's was conveniently placed between the Capitol Building and the White House. Kimberlee would be nearby to his kitchen no matter where she landed in DC. And knowing her, once she set a goal there was no stopping the woman. Maybe he should aim to be White House chef someday.

9

"Your belly would be gi-normous if it wasn't hidden in so much fur, Zackie."

The Sheltie settled into her doggie front seat with a sigh of perfect contentment.

"Time to go see another friend," Dilya pulled away from Pauley's Island and began winding her way out of DC.

Do not look local, Suyuan had said. *If she in trouble, she not leave any footprints here. Not in DC.*

Then where? Dilya had nearly cried aloud.

There is librarian network—all special librarians.

Dilya knew what that was. There were public librarians, government, and corporate. Then there were the special librarians. They handled unique collections, like Suyuan's tea collection or Miss Watson's spy-craft library. DC probably had more special librarians than most other cities in the world. But if Suyuan was right, then the locals couldn't help her.

We stay in touch. Maybe she leave a message for you at special library.

But there are thousands. Where was she supposed to begin?

League of Nations. The library of President Woodrow Wilson's attempt to build the League of Nations out of World War I was housed in the UN Building in New York.

Dilya had sat clenching her empty teacup in the serenity of Ching Ching CHA, amazed that it didn't shatter in her grasp. *Why?*

Your friend, Suyuan had insisted, *she often talked about how it was the first beginning. The first try to make peace for world.*

As Dilya rolled past the White House, which was no longer her home, she couldn't help thinking about how far the world had strayed from that particular ideal.

Peace was also homeless these days.

"It's just us, Zackie." Her dog didn't wake.

But that wasn't right. Unlike when she'd hiked across the Hindu Kush alone at age nine, she now had a family. And many friends, more than she'd ever imagined with the help of the special librarians network.

And was it merely coincidence that one of the Chef's Club now worked at the UN?

PART THREE

THE CATALOG MESSAGE

1

VALENTINA MOREAU CHECKED HER PHONE FOR ABOUT THE hundredth time. Still no messages since the one that had slammed in last night and destroyed any chance of sleep.

Must visit Dag Hammarskjöld Library. Help!

They'd stayed in touch through college, though rarely seen each other since high school.

It was the *Help!* that was so startling. Dilya Stevenson had always been the one to *provide* help, never needing anything from any of the rest of their old Chef's Club group. She'd given friendship, cautious at first but finally with all her heart.

That was the only thought that made Val smile this morning as she'd brushed her teeth in her small third-floor walk-up in Brooklyn. She wondered if that thought might surprise Dilya. Not much did, but Val suspected that would.

Downstairs she'd greeted the landlords who occupied the rest of the old brownstone as they returned from their morning walk with their rangy mutt. Mokey was big for a New York dog, but they walked him a lot, which was nice. Val gathered her usual black coffee and bagel with just a shmear of plain cream cheese—salmon cream cheese was for the weekends when she wasn't in face-to-face meetings for much of the day.

She congratulated herself on how well she was settling into New York life only three months out of college. Her timing was good and she caught the Carroll Street F-train after only a few minutes on the underground platform.

Help! It was that exclamation point that was so unusual. Dilya was always the calm center of any storm—completely unflappable. Working and living in the White House all through her teen and college years as First Nanny and First Dog buddy, meant she'd seen some serious storms.

The F-train squealed through the York Street curve before ducking under the East River. She was careful to meet the eyes of only the few she recognized as regulars. New York was not Paris or DC where she'd spent her youth and her teens—people here were unknowns. Like most subway commuters, she wore obvious ear buds. Probably unlike most, hers and Dilya's were never playing anything.

Dilya had taught them all a sense of *cautious paranoia.* Val tried to think of it in Dilya's way, *missed opportunities for information,* but rarely succeeded. The girl seemed to hear everything everywhere, though she didn't often share it. Val had never shaken off the time she'd been attacked in the high school locker room, or that Dilya had been the one to save her. And she'd forced Val to press charges—over eighteen, he'd done jail time.

She missed the Broadway and Lafayette Street change to the east side trains and had to stay on until Bryant Park at 42nd Street. She couldn't even remember the weather up above. Was she in for a wet walk cross-town? No, Mokey's fur had been dry. And it was still September, a lovely time of year in the city.

During the long walk across half the width of Manhattan, she had to exercise special care. The food cart vendors were already out and she tended to be a compulsive eater when she was nervous.

Help!

Giant pretzels, donuts, more bagels, chili dogs, falafels, Viet noodles... Suddenly everything looked scrumptious, yet telling her nerves that her stomach wasn't hungry didn't slow them down at all. Telling herself she was in danger of running late, she hurried onward.

By pure willpower she managed to reach the security gate to the United Nations Buildings at precisely five to nine, right on schedule, with no extra calories. She would be at her desk as the intern to the French UN Ambassador by nine sharp. Though it would be useless, as she knew she wouldn't do anything useful until Dilya finally arrived.

2

THE UN HAD ALWAYS BEEN ONE OF HER BETTER COUPS; DILYA smiled as she and Zackie approached the security gates. A quick text to Val from two blocks out meant they should arrive at the gates at the same moment.

She knew this ground well, though she was used to whisking in with a Secret Service detail, not walking the four blocks from the nearest parking garage. The former First Lady, now Mrs. Secretary of State, wasn't the least bit overshadowed by her President-husband. As the World Heritage Convention Ambassador to the UN, Geneviève Matthews ranked as a powerhouse in her own right. She was *the* international advocate for all UNESCO World Heritage Sites—the ambassador of UNESCO to all UN ambassadors.

Dilya's coup had been back when she was the First Nanny. She'd become a fixture beside First Lady Geneviève Matthews as she cornered one country's ambassador after another at the United Nations. Or internationally as she visited world leaders to drive her agenda. When the incoming First Lady had been recruited as Genny's assistant specializing in the natural rather than manmade World Heritage sites, Dilya had already been a fixture. Zackie, the new First Dog, quickly became one as well.

But that was behind her now. As of five days ago, she was no longer the First Nanny. And the First Lady had given Zackie to Dilya, keeping one of Zackie's puppies for herself. She still hadn't had time to think about that change.

She and Zackie arrived at the security gate in mid-town Manhattan where the United States of America ended and the United Nations began. It was the one tiny enclave in the whole country that didn't belong to the United States; these few square blocks along the East River belonged to the world.

Her arrival was carefully timed to ten a.m. because that's when there was the lowest foot traffic here, after the workers' arrivals but before most diplomats were on the move. She'd wanted to be able to see if anyone was following her but, if so, she couldn't pick them out.

"Dilya!" Val breezed up to the security checkpoint. Valentina Moreau never moved any other way. She was everything Dilya wasn't: tall, blonde, and elegantly French. Dilya's average height, dark ruffled hair that never behaved, and Uzbekistani tan-dark skin simply couldn't compare. And Val's inner composure was even more daunting, which had always left Dilya feeling hesitant around her.

But Val's hug was unstinting and enveloped Dilya as softly as the cheek-to-cheek pair of French air kisses that proceeded it. She'd been like this in high school and Dilya had never stopped being surprised by her Old-World manners. All of the others kids just said, *Hey!* if they spoke to her at all. Even in the heart of DC, being that *one who worked in the White House* had been the mark of strangeness that she'd only breached with her four friends from the

Chef's Club. It had never helped that whenever the news mentioned her, it was always as *the adopted war orphan,* often not mentioning her name at all.

The four Chef's Club members had become Dilya's close friends, in fact her only friends of her own age. And though they'd gone their own ways for and since college, now she needed their help.

"I don't know if I can get you onto the grounds. Definitely not with your dog. I am but an intern to the French UN ambassador."

"Oh, that won't be a problem." Dilya reached into her pack and tugged out a service dog vest. In moments she had it snapped around the little Sheltie's chest.

"You can't simply make things up, Dilya. They will check."

Dilya tickled Zackie's ears. "That's fine. Zackie is a trained and certified service dog. The harness is only to stop questions." Zackie was the perfect decoy. The small dog had been trained, with the assistance of the Secret Service dog handlers, to be far more than she appeared. The three of them walked up to the security gate.

"Hello, Miss Stevenson. And how is Zackie today?" The woman guard held out a dog biscuit which Zackie took politely. Crunching sounds punctuated the rest of their brief conversation.

Val watched the goings-on with wide eyes.

"He's doing fine, Ms. James. How are the boys?" Dilya handed over her White House ID that she hadn't turned in when she'd quit working there. Of course, the First Lady was the only one who knew she'd quit five days ago, and most of her belongings were still in the bedroom deep in the Residence. As First Nanny, she'd primarily lived in the Residence.

"Do *not* get me started. In my next lifetime, I'm only having girls. I swear." She rested her hand on her chest in solemn oath, before handing over an all-areas visitor badge. "Any chance I could trade them in on the two of you?"

Val smiled uncertainly.

"Three of us, Ms. James," she nodded toward Zackie.

"It would still be a bargain. Though Herman would not be pleased. But that won't stop this gal from wishin'." She heaved an overly dramatic sigh and smiled before turning to the next person arriving at her booth.

"What was that about?" Val asked as soon as they were in the clear and following the sidewalk through the UN grounds. They passed the long low General Assembly building. The outside appeared to be blah-concrete, which was funny as most people would recognize the interior massive circular meeting room that could host all the world's nations at once. The glass tower of the Secretariat soared thirty-nine stories above the small park at the center of the grounds. Dilya had been in its underground stories as well, which contained security, private meeting rooms, and emergency shelters.

"Her twin boys are high school seniors and captains of two different sports teams. She's supposed to go to all of their games, which chews up every minute she isn't here."

"Why does Herman not like dogs? Which one is he?"

"Herman is actually a she. When they were little, the boys misnamed her for Hermione from Harry Potter. She's a cat and doesn't like dogs of any size. A knee-high Sheltie definitely wouldn't rate. Sorry, Zackie."

The Sheltie smiled up at her and padded happily alongside. Zackie wasn't exactly fond of cats either so it all worked out.

Val studied her for a long moment with her bright blue

eyes. Dilya had always envied her those, but to little avail. Her own eyes remained as relentlessly soft green as her body remained...not tall and blonde. She was mostly over that. The lead helicopter pilot that had rescued her from the depths of the Afghan War had been as tall and blonde as Val.

Except Val had a softness—and Emily Beale was pure warrior steel.

Dilya had always wanted to be like Emily in every way she could even before she could speak her language. When she had learned it, she'd cultivated Emily's Mid-Atlantic accent rather than her adoptive mother's rapid East LA, though she could do that fluently—and a dozen other regional accents as well. It was a useful skill sometimes.

They walked in silence along the circular drive that led from the front gate to the tower's entrance.

It was one of Val's gifts, making silence comfortable. There were a hundred things whirling about in Dilya's head at any given minute of the day. And twice that now with Miss Watson gone missing. Val somehow created silence.

3

VAL WATCHED DILYA, BUT SHE'D GIVEN NO INDICATION OF WHY they had to meet since her desperate text message.

From the very first day when they'd all met in the White House kitchen, Dilya had always been the one who could do anything, get anywhere. Now Val had a glimpse of how Dilya did it and, as always, it made her feel slow— something only Dilya could do to her.

Val had worked here at the UN for the two months since graduating from Oxford. Unlike some, Val was always polite to the security guards, but she'd never thought to learn their names or anything about their families.

Whether Dilya had done it out of kindness or some convoluted master plan to prepare for a moment like this was one of the questions Val had always wondered but never dared ask. Dilya had become far too important a friend to risk discovering that Val herself was also part of some hidden Dilya agenda.

Val had founded the Chef's Club as a way to gather out-of-the-box thinkers from the different cliques in high school. She'd become desperately bored by the pretty-girl set that insisted on making her their queen bee. Instead, she'd gathered three others who were all top students but had been as trapped by their roles as she had: the jock, the brainy socialite, and the nerd. The jock was also the son of one of Washington DC's top chefs, which had given her the idea of being together to visit professional kitchens in the city for cooking and culture classes.

As they moved across the central paved park, Dilya was greeted several more times. No one appeared to notice Val close beside her.

It was Dilya Stevenson who had set fire to the group. They'd continued to visit world-class kitchens, but they'd also begun taking their own cultural ideas, honing them into political ones, and sometimes suggesting them to their various connections. As a behind-the-scenes group, they had sparked two different bills into Congress through Kimberlee's Senator-father. Val's own father had taken three of the group's suggestions back to the French in his role as the embassy's defense attaché. Dilya had the ear of the Oval Office, which had been quite the most staggering of all.

Dilya had even arranged a social meeting with the President in the Oval Office, and another with the former President. It had been his story of how he'd first met his future wife at the UN that had finally set Val's path toward that target. Not that she was husband hunting, but rather the way he had described the power and strength of his Viet-French wife dominating a meeting. Val wanted to be like that even though she knew she was far too timid. Without Dilya, she'd never have tried.

Dilya and Zackie passed through the main lobby and the internal security checkpoint with the same ease that they had at the outer gate. She didn't know the guard, the man was new, but by the time they'd been passed inward,

Val felt as if they'd become good acquaintances headed toward friendship.

And, as Dilya had said, nobody bothered about Zackie at all, though Val was fairly certain she was the only dog in the whole UN other than a seeing-eye dog for a Danish translator.

Neither of them spoke until they were at the threshold of the vast main hall of the Dag Hammarskjöld Library itself. She led Dilya over to her favorite chairs. A small group of four armchairs in the far corner of the library's ground floor hall. She loved this corner as she alone, perhaps of anyone here, knew by President Matthews's own words that her was where he had first met Geneviève Beauchamp.

"So, why are we here? And why do you need my help?"

4

___

DILYA WISHED SHE KNEW. SHE GRABBED VAL'S HAND BRIEFLY
and squeezed it hard to make sure her friend was real—and
to calm herself with the contact. In the last five days she'd
had little sleep and none of it restful.

Val was real.

Dilya dropped into one of the well-worn brown-leather
armchairs. There were several other groups in the long
room, chatting in the comfortable chairs, but none nearby.

Zackie veered over toward the card catalog. Dilya had to
snap her fingers twice and point at the floor between the
chairs before Zackie settled by their feet. They needed to
keep a low profile.

She'd enjoy the comfort of having Zackie in her lap, but
the dog vest had been built to Secret Service specs complete
with bulletproof Kevlar and a lifting handle. There were
even the fittings for a remote camera that could feed to her
phone and some other hidden electronics like a
microphone that transmitted to her phone with an
encrypted signal—very convenient for sending the dog to
eavesdrop on conversations she couldn't enter herself. All of

the technology made the vest uncomfortable with Zackie in her lap.

She glanced around the library. It was a favorite unofficial meeting place at the UN. Groups of chairs had replaced most of the standard library tables. The broad windows of the Dag Hammarskjöld's card catalog room offered a lovely view of the pretty side of the General Assembly Building. Here, the wood-paneled ceiling formed into a wave-like flowing curve, invited the eye to wander upward and outward. The old card catalog of the original League of Nations ranged down the length of an entire wall, though here and there leather chairs had now been backed up against it.

It was hardly a physical library at all anymore. She could search the catalog remotely on her phone and request titles that were stored in the basement levels below. But it was a vast collection and she didn't know where to begin.

"Miss—" No. Even here she shouldn't say the name aloud. "My friend from the basement."

Val nodded her understanding because she never missed any nuance in any conversation or event. If anything, she had the opposite problem. She was so sensitive that she often saw veiled intentions where there really weren't any.

Miss Watson had been Dilya's mentor for years. An ex-master spy, overseeing an archive of spycraft lore and especially the history of every known female spy, had been ensconced in the White House Residence's lowest subbasement since before Dilya had found Val. Or rather Miss Watson had found her.

"She's gone," Dilya told Val in a normal voice, knowing that whispers would attract more attention. "Truly gone. Her, the library—no trace. I saw her ten days ago. Five days ago, gone."

Val's surprise was absolutely genuine though she revealed it with no more than a lift of her eyebrows. "And why did that lead you here?"

"I saw Kimberlee in Alabama. She suggested I follow the library itself because there would be no way to follow the woman. Especially if she's in as much trouble as I fear. In DC, Trevor led me to a tea librarian who suggested I begin my search here."

"I didn't know there was such a thing as a tea librarian."

"Neither did I until yesterday."

Val scanned the room. "Start here? You think you're going to find your...friend's small library within this one? Do you know how big this library is?"

Dilya shook her head. "I never paid much attention to it."

5

"What—" But Val stopped herself. Asking what Dilya *had* paid attention to at the UN might lead them along deep and strange pathways. Dilya had asked for help and she would do her best to give it.

By her watch, she had an hour before she was to attend a UN staff training session that apparently the French UN ambassador himself had set up. She'd already done the preparation last week and could probably teach the class herself, but she would behave and appear attentive without using much of her attention. Her conversations with Dilya always required her fullest attention.

"This library contains eighty thousand maps in a wide variety of languages. It contains the complete archives of the UN and the League of Nations. That card catalog," she gestured to the back wall where the ten-tier card catalog stretched the entire length of the room, "is for the League of Nations. There's another one on the floor above for the non-digitized portion of UN proceedings from 1945 to 1992 in the six official languages of the UN—they're about halfway through scanning and coding the twenty million documents there. Everything since 1992 is digital and you can ask the online system, called *Ask DAG,* to research it. There are about a bazillion levels of basements for storing the books and documents."

Dilya collapsed into her chair eliciting a worried whine from Zackie. Several delegates from Eastern Europe glanced over from their meeting at a nearby table and quickly looked away.

Val reached down to rub Zackie's ears and whispered a soft, "Hush."

The dog quieted instantly but kept her eyes trained on Dilya.

Then Val started to laugh softly.

"What?" Dilya squinted at her.

"We're in a library."

"So?"

"Let's ask the librarian."

Dilya's fierce hug took her completely by surprise, as did most things with her friend.

6

"I'm new here," the head librarian had been easy to find, working in his second floor office. "They only hired me last week. The position came open very unexpectedly."

"Why was that?" Val asked when Dilya didn't speak.

Dilya hadn't even been able to open her mouth or form a coherent question. Every time she began to hope, that hope was dashed aside. His being here less than a week, meant that this head librarian hadn't started until after Miss Watson had disappeared from her basement hideaway. Or was it at the same moment?

"What was your previous position?" Dilya cut the man off before he could answer Val's question.

"Director of the California Digital Library for the UC system. Is this a job interview? I already have a job." His smile was as pleasant and easygoing as the man himself.

Dilya considered. They'd found his office off the second floor of the Dag library. It was relatively small and nondescript for such a prestigious position. Of course, time and the relative success of the UN had added a great deal of pressure to the original space. There were now two skyscrapers off-campus across First Avenue that were part of the UN. And they were seeking permission to build a new building to the south because they no longer really fit into the existing space.

There was a desk, several guest chairs, and a three-screen computer system worthy of the Situation Room reference desks run by the National Security Council. His walls were blank, though a few picture frames were propped against the wall but as yet unhung.

Why was he humoring them? They were a pair of twenty-one-year-olds and a dog, not the ambassador to India or some such.

Then his computer's screensaver kicked in—his arm reaching out to take a selfie of himself and two grinning kids. His daughter could be Valentina Moreau's younger twin, which answered that question.

"To address your implied question, I wanted to move to New York because my family is here." And by his grimace as he said that, Dilya decided it was his *ex-wife* and children who were here, a fact supported by the screen's image. Then he turned to Val, "To answer your direct question, it was because of the death of the previous librarian."

7

VAL HAD WANTED TO USE THE COMPUTERS IN THE LIBRARY, she'd also offered the one at her cube-desk.

Dilya declined. Miss Watson's training in spycraft had made her far too conscious of possible electronic surveillance. She certainly didn't want to draw unwelcome attention to her friend or the helpful librarian either.

Val had to head off to her training session in diplomatic security, which sounded as if they were already grooming her for a better position (no surprise to Dilya). Val gave a light scoff when Dilya mentioned it.

"We are all very worried about security here at the UN. My father talks of when he first came here, he barely had to show his personal identification. Now it requires a UN pass or an escort. There are metal detectors, sniffing guard dogs, and cybersecurity. Nobody just walks in here the way you did."

"My White House pass is a little special." It had to be as First Nanny. She could enter the Oval during a meeting, had been in the Situation Room several times, and could carry a knife in the presence of the President, which she did whenever they were out of the White House. Technically, she could probably carry a firearm as well, but she'd never liked guns. That was her sniper-stepmom's specialty.

With Val busy, Dilya opted for a Starbucks—there was nowhere more anonymous. She headed across town. After passing three different Starbucks, she doubled back and chose the one closest to the UN.

New York's daily streets were worse than DC's at the height of the tourist season. The foot traffic was so dense on the sidewalks that it was impossible to tell if she was being followed. On the plus side, in turn it made her almost impossible to follow.

A tall hot chocolate for her and a Puppucino for Zackie. The Sheltie had a major weakness for the freebie cup of whipped cream they offered to dogs, and never failed to look at her in question every time her sensitive nose passed within blocks of a Starbucks. Dilya never had to look for their location, all she had to do was nod permission and Zackie would lead her straight to the nearest one. It had taken a while to train her *not* to trigger at every pedestrian with a to-go cup in their hands.

While Zackie lay under the chair, her Puppucino cup pinned between her forepaws as her tongue darted in and out, Dilya made sure her back was to a wall to ensure that no one could see over her shoulder. She logged in using a VPN to reach out to a bank of computers that the Secret Service kept running with the sole purpose of secure communications. Keying in her RSI code, her query became untraceable.

Librarian deaths. She'd meant to add *at the UN,* but Zackie bumped her leg as she rolled over for a nap after finishing her cup of whipped cream. Dilya hit the Enter key by mistake.

The search engine announced several million results but the first was the American Libraries magazine obituaries page which sounded promising. The list was fifty-seven pages and twelve years long.

She flipped screens until she hit three weeks ago and spotted the *UN* in one of the obits. That gave her the name, and she searched on that. The head librarian at Dag hadn't merely died, she'd been murdered. Nothing was taken, she was simply dead on the sidewalk three blocks from the UN. The police had decided it was a mugging gone wrong.

Other searches brought up more librarians dead under suspicious circumstances. A burst of laughter from a nearby table had her flinching until she saw it was a group of old Italian men telling each other stories over coffee. They looked as if they'd been planted there every morning since time began.

A quick scan of the coffee shop revealed no one watching her, simply the constant ebb and flow of orders, the auto-grinder chewing up more beans, and the hot hisses from the baristas' machines as they made the five hundredth cappuccino of the morning.

Dilya returned her attention to the librarians' deaths. She spent an hour ferreting through the lists, narrowing criteria and building a list, until she had five of them.

All head librarians.

All were in charge of special collections rather than being public or university librarians. The UN librarian in New York, two in DC, one in London, and one in Geneva.

All in the last six months.

And all of them were about Miss Watson's age.

What if—

The next search revealed that they'd all gone through the University of Washington's library school in the 1970s.

And immediately after grad school, they all had a significant gap in their history, as if they'd...

"What?" she asked her computer. "Ceased to exist for a decade or two?"

One of the old Italians looked at her strangely as the group rose to their feet. But in moments he was gone and the table quickly filled with three intense looking millennials who didn't appear to know each other but set to work intently on their separate computers. By the speed each was typing, they were drinking triple espresso shots in their Nitro Cold Brews.

She was too used to talking aloud to Zackie when she was trying to figure something out. She clamped her mouth shut.

What could make a librarian disappear from public record?

Of them all, only Miss Watson had no history at all past grad school. That made perfect sense because she'd become a spy for the CIA.

Oh! Dilya wanted to smack her forehead. They'd all been spies. Together.

Who else had been recruited from the class? She couldn't see any way to find out.

She downloaded their obituaries and then thought to search for Miss Watson's.

Nothing.

Then she tried Miss Watson's original name, wondering how many people knew it.

Please don't let me find it. Please. Please. Ple—

Dilya almost screamed aloud when it popped up, until she spotted the date. Miss Watson had let the CIA think she was dead over twenty years before, and there was the brief obituary for *Emmaline Trask* to support that.

Several warnings flashed up on her screen. A cyber sniffer had been triggered and was trying to find her. Blocked at the Secret Service's computer in DC.

Dilya dumped her connection. And her system informed her she was out clean.

But someone, who knew Miss Watson's real name, now knew that someone else was looking for her.

That sniffer attack did tell Dilya one thing: Miss Watson was still alive and whoever had set up the alert on that old obituary wanted to find her very badly. And probably for other reasons than renewing old college friendships.

Dilya could only hope that she hadn't made matters worse for Miss Watson...wherever she was. Please let her be safe.

8

———

"You were right. How are you always right?" Val sighed as she rejoined Dilya and her dog in the back corner of the Dag Hammarskjöld main room.

"Trust me, I'm not."

"You so are. The security training was for UN protocols on top of the security clearance I already had for being the daughter of the French Defense Attaché. I am no longer an intern but now one of the French UN ambassador's assistants."

"It doesn't surprise me at all," Dilya smiled at her as she scratched Zackie's ears. The dog had snuggled up in the chair beside Dilya. She'd always been so slender that they weren't crowded in the armchair. *The wonders of a starvation diet,* she'd always say when asked. She'd never had enough food until she was rescued at eleven, by then her body was set in its ways.

"It would surprise me, if it weren't for what Miss Wa—" Val caught herself. "For what your friend once told me."

"What was that?" Dilya leaned forward eagerly as if

greedy for any word of her missing mentor, even a past word.

"She said I had the elegance and the brains to be a great peacemaker one day."

"Duh."

Val actually laughed because she didn't know what else to do. "Why is this so obvious to everyone but me?"

Dilya just shrugged.

"She gave me all of these crazy books to read. Biographies. Eleanor Roosevelt, Michelle Obama, Missy LeHand who was kind of the first-ever White House Chief of Staff to Franklin Roosevelt. And not only politics. Hedy Lamarr was one of those long ago movie stars, who invented all sorts of things that now make everything from torpedoes to cell phones work. Like I could ever be like one of those women."

"Or maybe because you so could be one of those women."

Dilya didn't make it a question and Val couldn't manage a scoff this time. It was too crazy.

"You've met the former First Lady, Geneviève Matthews, right? Elegant, brilliant, French-Vietnamese, so you have a partially shared heritage there."

"And *terrifant.*"

Dilya blinked at her in surprise. "She's not terrifying, she's amazing. And you are so much like a blonde version of her. Miss W was absolutely right about you, Val. Now you have to own it. That's your challenge."

"I'm just me, not some Olypmic superstar." Val wondered what it would feel like to have that kind of confidence.

"Says you." Dilya waved toward the middle of the room.

Val turned to see what had caught her attention.

There, rising from another group of seats, Geneviève Matthews returned Dilya's wave and headed in their direction.

"Good morning, ladies. What brings you to the UN today?"

Before Val could speak, which she wasn't sure if she could manage even if given the chance, Dilya jumped in.

"Hello, Genny. You remember Val from the Chef's Club? She's an assistant to the French UN ambassador. I'm only visiting."

"*Merveilleuse.* Of course I remember. You asked my husband many interesting questions." Her hand rested lightly on Val's shoulder as they exchanged a pair of *la bise* air kisses exactly as she'd greeted Dilya. "I must rush off, but will you be here for lunch tomorrow?"

Dilya shrugged her uncertainty, but Val could only nod. Where else would she be?

"*Parfaite!* Then at least we two girls must meet. Here at one?" She addressed Val. Without waiting for more than Val's mechanical nod of consent, she waved her hand and was gone.

Val twisted to face Dilya, "What have you just done to me?"

"You want a mentor in how to become who you already are? You now have it. Trust me, she's awesome. She's the one who first brought me to the White House."

Val could only stare in horror. But she could also feel a smile coming on. Friends with the official ambassador for the UN's World Heritage Centre and her ex-President husband who was now Secretary of State? Maybe it wasn't Val about to become Miss Watson's *Great Peacemaker*. What if it was Dilya?

It was moments like this that her friend appeared to spawn with such perfect ease that made her so amazing.

Except Dilya wasn't the least bit at ease.

"What's up, Dilya?"

9

DILYA EXPLAINED ABOUT THE LIBRARIAN DEATHS SHE'D uncovered and watched Val's cheeks go even paler than they'd been when Genny had come over to their corner.

When she shooed Zackie out of the chair for cuddling too close in her bulletproof vest, Zackie walked over and sat in front of the card catalog.

Dilya pulled up the obits as Val slid her chair tight against her own and they began reading through them together. Each death was different and could be dismissed as chance: car accident, drowning, small plane crash...

Taken together though, with the added university and history gap, it made a scary pattern. Someone with a long and powerful reach was hunting the classmates-turned-spy from Miss Watson's library school. And there was a good chance that's why she'd disappeared so abruptly and with so little trace. Miss Watson was on the run for her very life.

"If she'd left an obvious clue for you," Val kept her voice low, "you might have tried to go straight to her. Maybe she was afraid that you were being watched as well."

"Am I being followed now, do you think? I already

bought a new phone with a new number and mailed the old one to Alaska. I even packed it with a long-life battery so that if someone traces it, they'll go on a wild goose chase."

"I wouldn't have thought of that. But I'm training to be a diplomat, not a spy."

"Is that what I am?" Dilya had never thought of it that way.

Val laughed in her face. "If there was ever anyone who could be anything, it is you, Dilya Stevenson."

She'd never thought of it that way either. Until five days ago, she'd always been comfortable in her role at the White House.

"You know, there's something about these obituaries…"

Dilya looked back at the screen, but noticed Val was staring out the towering floor-to-ceiling windows at the ebb and flow of cars allowed onto the inner circular drive. She stared as well and noticed that there was a rising influx of vehicles compared to this morning. There must be an upcoming meeting at the General Assembly building that dominated the far side of the traffic circle.

"There is…" Val was squinting now. "Ah, they were all written by the same person."

"They were?"

"Yes," Val nodded her certainty. "I often proofread the memos and letters from the French UN ambassador's office. I can tell which of the staff has written each one, even when they're in the ambassador's name. These are all the same."

Dilya opened the last one, the obituary of the Dag Hammarskjöld's librarian and began reading. As she did, she could actually hear Miss Watson's voice in her head. And, as in each of the others, the missing years were glossed over as if they'd never been.

"That's odd," Val pointed to the end of the document. She'd always been a fast reader.

Dilya followed her finger to last line: *She was always proud of the chefs she knew.* But there wasn't a single other word about chefs or cooking in the whole obituary.

"She's talking to us!" Val insisted when Dilya shook her head to clear it.

"She was...proud...of the Chef's Club. Not the dead librarian, but Miss W. But there's nothing else here." Dilya reread the last few paragraphs but didn't see any further clues.

Zackie whined loudly enough to get her attention.

"*Sàmhach,*" she ordered in Scottish Gaelic. It had seemed only appropriate to train a Sheltie in the language of Shetland.

Zackie quieted but didn't look away from the card catalog.

With a sudden itch between her shoulder blades, Dilya rose and crossed to the dog. It felt as if she was moving in slow motion. Zackie was low to the ground and the card catalog wasn't, so it was hard to tell exactly where she was looking.

But she and Val had been sitting at the beginning, close by the As. Zackie was fixated on the middle of the Cs and it wasn't hard to guess which one.

Of its own will, her hand reached out and pulled open the drawer marked *Chas-Cheh.* Hundreds of cards filled the long drawer, each one typewritten by some long-ago librarian creating title cards for every volume in the collection.

At the back—where room had been left to expand if more cards were added—there was a strip of beef jerky. She sniffed it. No scent of spices or salt. Beef jerky for dogs.

She handed it to Zackie, who lay down and began chewing away happily.

Val stepped up beside her and began flipping cards. "Um, it goes straight from *Cheetahs* to *Chefchaouen,* which is apparently a city in Morocco. No *Chefs.*"

Dilya braced herself against the catalog. The dog treat. Miss Watson had banked on her coming here, to this library, with Zackie, to find this very drawer. But there was nothing to be found. Had the librarian killer already been here and taken the next clue?

Val moved over to check the *Clu* drawer for *Clubs* but only shook her head.

Why had Miss Watson laid such an obscure trail?

Duh! Because after seeing so many of her friends killed over the last six months, she was afraid for her life.

So, what was the next level of obfuscation?

As Dilya thought it, she looked up. At waist level were five tiers of card catalog drawers by title. But card catalogs were double-enteried. Every item cataloged in a library must also be traceable by subject. And at shoulder level were five more tiers of drawers by subject.

She selected the one that would include *Chef* and there it was.

Chef's Club. One card only. The lower edge of the index stock had been notched to fit tightly around a central metal rail that kept the cards from sliding out of place. She freed it from the tray with a slight yank. She checked the cards before and after, but they appeared to be unrelated.

Then she focused on the card. Lines of symbols.

"It's covered with code," Val looked over her shoulder.

"I was never particularly good with codes. I simply can't get the hang of them. You?"

Val shook her head, "But I know who is."

10

―――――

By the time Val had pushed the drawer closed, Dilya had her laptop stuffed into her bag and had gathered her other belongings from the table.

"Wait, where are you going?"

"To find Jimmy. He was the king of codes in our group," she was tapping away on her phone.

"But—"

Her phone pinged. "How far away is Conway, New Hampshire?"

"I don't know, it's—" she waved her hand toward the north.

As usual, Dilya was five steps ahead of her. "I can drive there in under eight hours. No. I have to get some sleep."

"You can—"

"I'll get past halfway before nightfall and I can be there in the morning."

—*stay with me.* It would have been nice. Val'd had a half-second image of a quiet evening with a good friend.

Somehow reading her mind in her Dilya way, her friend

grabbed her in another one of her fierce hugs. "I'll come to visit once I know Miss W is safe. I promise."

"I'll—" *look forward to it.* But Dilya was gone with Zackie fast on her heels.

Val straightened the chairs and then started with shock.

Tomorrow! Lunch! Geneviève Matthews!

How could Dilya leave her alone for such a meeting?

If Dilya could take on the world to find and perhaps rescue Miss Watson, perhaps Val could manage to survive tomorrow's lunch.

But then she thought about how she'd come to this place. Her determination to be like the woman President Matthews so respected. The French UN ambassador promoting her so quickly. Those books, those great piles of books Miss Watson had recommended over the years. And Dilya's fierce belief in her.

Perhaps tomorrow's lunch wasn't only terrifying.

It was also an opportunity.

Val squared her shoulders, made sure that her dress was neat and her long hair still hung in a clean fall.

Maybe she already was good enough for whatever came next.

Peacemaker material.

Valentina Moreau liked the sound of that. A lot.

PART FOUR

THE RAILWAY CODE

1

———

DILYA STEVENSON RAN OUT OF STEAM WHEN SHE REACHED
Conway, New Hampshire. In the last six days, had she
slept...as many hours? She must have, but didn't remember
them. Or feel them.

Technically, she ran out of useful consciousness at the
Conway Scenic Railroad's station in North Conway. A large
village green formed the center of town. To the right ranged
a line of tourist shops, long since closed for the night, and a
few bars and restaurants, still doing late business.

To her left, across the green, stood a train station that
looked as if someone had teleported it brand-new out of the
eighteen hundreds. A fanciful structure, mustard yellow
with twin towers of red, white, and black, it reached up into
the darkness. She pulled over and clambered out of her
Mini Cooper.

Zackie, her Sheltie, had slept most of the long drive from
the United Nations building in New York and bounded out
with annoying energy.

She leaned her forehead against the darkened window

of the station. A gift shop, filled with model trains and t-shirts.

And no people. There were security lights, but the place was closed.

Circling behind the station, a strange collection of passenger trains confronted her. Big diesel engines, an all-black steam engine, and a collection of classic Pullman cars that boasted high-polish wood and brass-bright fittings lined up on the tracks. A mash-up of the twentieth and nineteenth centuries. Maybe the eighteenth? What did an Uzbekistani war orphan know about American railcars?

Lines of pert tables and seats were visible through the broad glass windows of the Pullmans. No bunks. If there had been, she'd happily crawl into one—if the doors weren't locked.

She sat on the bottom step of one of the engines, pulled out her phone, and texted Jimmy.

Where are you?

Hey Dilya, where are you?

At the train station.

Me too. Where?

Sitting on the step of an engine.

A long pause followed. Zackie swung by on her investigations, left a cold nose print on Dilya's arm, and disappeared once more into the darkness.

Can't find you. Which one?

She was too tired for games. *The big yellow dieselly one.*

We only have little engines. Then he continued with, *How big?*

I dunno. Train-engine sized.

You're in North Conway, aren't you?

So?

Her phone rang loud enough to make her yelp at the same time Zackie arrived mere steps ahead of a policeman.

"You're in the wrong station, Dilya," the phone broadcast on speaker. A bright work light behind him shadowed Jimmy's face.

"He's got that right, Miss," the officer answered. "Didn't you see the no trespassing sign?"

She shook her head at both of them.

Zackie sat on her feet. It was usually annoying as she typically did it moments before Dilya had to hurry off, causing her to trip at the most unexpected moments. Now it was the only thing anchoring her to the Earth. Her whole body buzzed with exhaustion.

"Dilya?" "Miss?"

"Where am I?"

"Conway Scenic Railway," everyone, including herself but thankfully not Zackie, said in unison. Because there it was, painted in gold lettering on every car.

"I'm at The *Cog* Railway," Jimmy said.

"That's an hour up the road, Miss," the officer said.

She knew that. She'd been at the Mount Washington Hotel at Bretton Woods when a state-sponsored terrorist blew up half of the resort last year. Their attempt to destroy the global leaders attending the biggest economic conference since the one there at the end of World War II, had failed utterly thanks to an explosives-sniffing Corgi. The Cog Railway Base Station lay only a few miles behind the hotel.

"I'm too tired to go another ten feet." Then Dilya hung up the phone and pulled Zackie into her lap. All she wanted to do was curl up and hide—too exhausted to cry, which she never did anyway.

2

JIMMY HATED CALLING IN FAVORS. PARTICULARLY THIS ONE. But in late September, the height of New Hampshire leaf-peeping season, there wouldn't be a single room at any price in North Conway.

A quick check on Airbnb and a few other apps proved he was right.

He closed his eyes and punched in Marsha's number.

"Murglph?"

He checked his phone. Eleven at night. Crap! Marsha was a total early bird. Had to be with her job.

"Hey, Marsh. Jimmy Martin here."

"Jinfruee Marshan?"

"Yeah. Look. I've got a friend in a bind at Conway Station. Can you put them up for the night?"

"As cute as shoo?" Her voice still slurred, but headed toward coherence.

Jimmy considered. He'd had a mega-crush on Dilya Stevenson since the first time they'd met. She was intriguing, beautiful, and so damn smart. But she'd always been kind of standoffish—a good friend, but never anything more. Of course, that's all she was to anybody as far as he could tell. Just the way she was wired?

He'd met Marsha when he'd applied for jobs at both Conway Scenic Railroad and The Cog Railway, and she'd acted seriously put out when he accepted the latter offer.

"Yeah," Dilya would rank as the cutest woman ever born, if she wasn't quite so terrifyingly awesome. "But not your type, Marsh."

"Cute *is* my type," her voice was mostly clear now. And she was telling the truth. Even after turning down her job offer, she'd tried to take him home every time they ran into each other—which happened surprisingly often among the small community of locals. The guys at The Cog had laughed when he mentioned the story. *Ah, the Marsha experience. Has a thing for train guys. More powerful than a locomotive.* This from a bunch of railroad engineers who knew what that meant down to the last horsepower.

He didn't know from personal experience and was frankly glad he'd dodged that, so far. She'd made it clear that he wasn't getting off the hook by simply going to work on the Mount Washington Cog Railway. He never knew what to do with women—not in high school, not in college, and not now. But she was also the only person in North Conway whose number he had.

"My friend..." he carefully didn't say *female friend.* Because that would open the girlfriend question, which she definitely wasn't. It also might make Marsha hang up on him. "...is at the station. Can you go get them?"

"What's it worth to you, Jimmy Martin?"

"I'll be really grateful."

She made a happy humming noise. "Done."

He called back Dilya's number. An extreme close-up view of a dog's nose greeted him.

"Hi Zackie."

The dog yipped happily in recognition.

"Dilya."

One eye peered at him over her dog's nose.

"I've got someone coming to pick you up. You can crash on her sofa for tonight. I'd come get you, but no one else is around to drive your car back here. And I've got to be here early tomorrow."

" 'Kay. Fine. The officer will be happy." She turned the phone to show a policeman petting Zackie's head.

Leave it to Dilya to make friends with everyone she met.

For the second time tonight, Dilya hung up on him with no other comment.

3

"You're not the kind of cute I was promised."

Zackie growled at the woman's tone as Dilya blinked at the tall, shapely brunette but couldn't think of how to answer. She did rest a hand on the Sheltie's back to quiet her.

"Evening, Marsha." The policeman had sat on a steel bench opposite the train steps where Dilya perched. Whether to guard against her or to keep her company, it told her how quiet his usual beat was in this town.

"Evening, Joe. She in any trouble?"

"Nah. Just wiped out. Wanted to make sure she ended up safe. Besides, I figure we don't have that many more nights like this before fall ends, so I'm using her as an excuse to simply sit outside."

Marsha looked at her watch. "You're off soon. Say hey to the wife, will you?"

"You'll talk to her before I do. She's working the morning train, double shift as one of her waiters quit this afternoon. She's already sacked out."

"Oh man, that sucks. Damn summer help." She turned

to face Dilya. "You want a job on tomorrow's train? Standard waitress gig. You're pretty enough to earn serious tips. Your dog would get cuteness points too."

Dilya looked down at Zackie. Had she ever taken the Sheltie on a train? DC's Metro subway a few times. She'd been as well behaved there as anywhere else.

Going back and forth on a train. Not worried about ticking off the wrong person in the White House, where she'd been First Nanny and First Dog Handler until she quit six days ago. Not worried about what she'd missed during one meeting or another, that she wasn't supposed to be in anyway. Though Zackie or the First Kid usually smoothed her way into those.

It sounded nice. Tomorrow, she could...

But she couldn't!

She wasn't in New Hampshire for a train ride. She was here to follow a line of clues. At the moment, Dilya couldn't remember what they were, only that they'd led her here.

Miss Watson.

Oh, right.

Her missing ex-master-spy mentor.

In trouble.

Deep trouble.

Dilya shook her head. No part-time job on a railroad.

"Not a big talker, are you?" the brunette asked. Uh, Marsha. Right.

She tried shaking her head again because she wasn't.

"Got a name?"

She nodded, then realized how obnoxious that must appear. "Dilya Stevenson. This is Zackie."

"Hi, Dilya. Jimmy said you need a place to sleep. I've got a couch and you're welcome to it. I've got her, Joe. You can

—" Then she twisted back to face Dilya so abruptly that it triggered Zackie.

The knee-high Sheltie sprang to her feet and gave a full-throated snarl directed at the woman. Then broke into barking with all the ferocity of a ninety-pound German Shepherd war dog.

Dilya's training reacted to the warning.

With a swing of her arm up her back—she found nothing. She hadn't regularly worn her long Cold Steel knife there in over a year. She must be beyond tired to have reached for it. Too obvious, though she'd always liked the reach of the seven-inch blade.

With a flick of her wrist, she dropped the Recon 1 four-inch folding knife out of its forearm sheath and swung it open with a sharp snap. The black-anodized steel caught no light in the night except for the stainless steel of the razor-honed edge.

The policeman froze, then slapped for his sidearm.

"Whoa!" Dilya's brain finally kicked in. "Sàmhach!" She ordered the Sheltie to be quiet in Scots Gaelic.

Zackie stopped the barking, but still stood at full guard with teeth bared.

Then Dilya very slowly refolded her knife and made a show of putting it away as she watched Officer Joe's finger remain alongside the trigger guard of his Sig Sauer P320 rather than on the trigger. "Sorry. You startled me and my reflexes kicked in."

"Some goddamn reflexes. Pulling a knife on us?" Officer Joe didn't lower his weapon. "I'll take that."

Dilya dragged it out slowly, and handed it over, which caused him to remove the supporting hand from his sidearm, and he let his aim drift away from targeting her face at near point-blank range. He stood close enough that she could take it now—if she had to. The Secret Service had trained her well in disarming techniques, but that didn't seem to be a good move at the moment. And he'd probably end up shooting the pretty train in the process.

She glanced at Marsha who still watched her wide-eyed.

"What?"

"Dilya Stevenson. And Zackie."

"Yes. So?"

Marsha shook her head. "I'll be damned. Joe, give her back her knife."

"Why?"

Marsha smiled. "Because if you check her ID, I bet it'll knock you on your ass."

Dilya, riding on the last of the adrenaline before the after-shakes set in, returned the smile. She bet it would.

4

JIMMY HAD ONLY BEEN WORKING AT THE MOUNT WASHINGTON Cog Railway for three months. He'd stayed late at the station tonight with only his dog for company to study the engine manuals. His brakeman certification had been signed off, but he wanted engine driver as well, though that lay a long way off yet.

Who was he kidding?

He'd stayed late because of Dilya's text this afternoon asking where he was. He'd replied with North Conway because, being the newest on the crew, he was still at go-fer-drudge level. The fabrication shop in town had built them a special part that they'd sent him to fetch. He'd taken the opportunity to swing into the Old Village Bakery as well and buy a bag of his dog's favorite, fresh-baked biscuits.

He hadn't heard from her for most of the summer, then the message had popped in.

Where are you?

Flustered, he'd answered *Railroad. North Conway.*

Her near instant reply of *Be there soon* had done something to his brain. His hour-long drive from North

Conway to The Cog's station at the base of Mount Washington wasn't that twisty, but he'd nearly gone off the highway several times.

He'd thought about asking if *soon* meant minutes, hours, or days. But he'd never quite found the nerve to text her back. By the end of the day, he'd been a basket case and chosen to stay late rather than have to face himself in the silence of his one-room apartment in the nearby village of Carroll.

He also hadn't thought to correct his location. There had to be some way to stop messing up around Dilya Stevenson, but he hadn't found it yet.

Now she'd marooned herself in North Conway. And no way was he calling one of the guys for a midnight drive into town.

"*You* can't drive, can you?" He looked down at his dog, who merely smiled back.

What would Marsha do to Dilya?

He had to smile at that. Even out-on-her-feet tired, he'd match Dilya against anyone.

But what in the world she was doing in upstate New Hampshire, and with the First Dog? He couldn't begin to imagine.

5

MARSHA STARED AT HER COUCH.

The sun hadn't risen yet. But the sheet and blanket lay neatly folded. The dents of a body in the cushions were smoothed out as well. No sign that Dilya or her dog had ever been here except for a note that said, *Thanks. D&Z.*

Dilya and Zackie.

Crap! She'd known Jimmy came from DC by his resume. And she'd heard down the railway rumor mill that he'd been chummy with some serious players in high school. She'd figured, sure, like everyone in DC knew a congressional aide or something.

But the White House?

Marsha tossed a couple of Pop-Tarts into the toaster. All she had time for before she had to be on the train.

She'd have made time for more if Dilya had still been here. Marsha had been something of a White House freak since she was a kid. And Dilya? What a coup that would have been. She'd never been prominent at the White House, but Marsha had eventually picked up how often she appeared in photos of the First Family. In the background, but almost always there with the dog or one of the kids.

Dilya Stevenson had traveled everywhere and Marsha hadn't ever been farther than Boston.

The chance to hear some of the inside, behind-the-scenes stories had slipped out of her apartment as quietly as she'd arrived.

Marsha bit into a grape Pop-Tart, which dribbled onto her white blouse.

Crap! She really had to do laundry. Yesterday's was a no-go, stained with baby drool. Or the day before's, because it had a big grease smear from a patron's wheelchair while helping them onto the train. She finally found an acceptable one, by which time she'd have to run the four blocks to the station to get there on time. And since she was the boss of the passenger-side crew, being late looked shitty.

Her grape Tart was now cold and heating it would spread goo everywhere. She tossed a fresh brown sugar cinnamon into the microwave and hit it with three five-second blasts. Or did she do four?

It burned the roof of her mouth. She'd done four. Too hot. And much less crispy than a toaster. Too late.

She sandwiched it against the crispier but now cold grape one and hoped they balanced each other as she hurried out the door.

Perhaps she wouldn't get her pound of flesh from that seriously cute Jimmy Martin, but maybe she'd finagle a chance to talk to Dilya. After all, the Conway Scenic Railroad ran to within a few miles of The Cog. And they did owe her.

Marsha stumbled to a halt halfway across the green, started to take a bite, and only remembered at the last second to lean forward enough that the Pop-Tarts dribbled on the grass instead of her last clean blouse.

What did she have to look forward to? Another season riding the thirty-mile round trip traced by the *Mountaineer?* Another three hundred and sixty-five Pop-Tart breakfasts on the run to service another gazillion passengers?

On a train all day, every day. Yet she'd been nowhere.

Dilya Stevenson had been everywhere.

She could do that too, right?

"All it takes is leaving North Conway," she told the town as she hurried along its four downtown blocks.

The waiter who had quit yesterday, leaving Joe's wife a hand short with no notice had gone *somewhere,* hadn't he?

Marsha wouldn't do that. The Conway Scenic—from high school summer jobs to four years full time—had been good to her. And enough for her. At least not until she'd talked to Dilya and given proper notice.

But then?

She grinned to the south, where the sole highway led out of town, because from here pretty much everything except Montreal lay in that direction.

Yeah. A plan. That's what she needed. Even simply saying *South* made more of a plan than she'd had before now. Trains and cute boys suddenly weren't good enough for her.

She bit into her grape-sugar-cinnamon Pop-Tart sandwich. Thankfully, they sold Pop-Tarts everywhere, so she was set.

6

———————

TRUE TO HER WORD, DILYA SAT ON AN ENGINE—THIS TIME, the right one because it was here at The Cog Base Station. She and Zackie sat out on the service walkway of the M-5 *Metallak* biodiesel engine despite the morning chill. Metallak had been a noted peacemaker and the son of a local tribe's chief. He'd died five years before The Cog's conception in 1852.

The base station was chilly because it sat twenty-seven hundred feet up the mountainside. She had bundled up in a thick parka with the First Dog across her lap.

Jimmy glanced back at the parking lot. No motorcade. No green-and-white helicopters. No phalanx of Secret Service agents. Definitely not used to seeing her alone and unprotected like this.

Especially not alone. Even away from school, they'd almost always met with other members of the Chef's Club —a high school group that her guidance had turned into a small think tank. He hadn't understood that's what it was at the time, though he'd bet that Dilya had.

Other than that, she lived inside that protective bubble that encapsulated the White House and the First Family.

"Uh, hi." *Brilliant, Jimmy. Just freaking brilliant.*

"Trains?" was Dilya's sharp riposte. She'd never been much of a one for social niceties—extra words. They'd been officially deemed a waste of time except under extreme circumstances.

"Yeah. They're fascinating. We design and build our own here. Real-world engineering."

Her head tip, followed by a brief nod, gave him a burst of approval energy that wiped out his sleep-deprived state more effectively than the coffee and blueberry muffin that had started his morning...or rather ended this interminable night.

"What brings you here?"

"You." Her flat statement brought on a surge of hope that he quickly squashed. The likes of Dilya Stevenson weren't for a cop's son—especially not a dead cop's son.

Merle, who'd been off on his morning round of begging breakfast scraps from the rest of the early crew, bounded out of the main building. The Sheltie raced down the ramp from the back doors licking his chops in a way that said he'd scored something sugary. On rounding the end of the guard rail, he spotted Dilya. Or, more likely, Zackie.

He let out a sharp bark of surprise as he skidded to a four-pawed halt on the wet grass.

Zackie watched him, but didn't make a sound.

"Yours?" Dilya asked, as voluble as ever.

"Merle."

"Haggard? Or his coloring?" His Sheltie's coat consisted of a wild splotchy mix of black, tan, white, and light blue. A coloring called blue merle. It made a sharp contrast to Zackie's classic white-and-sable coloring.

He broke into the chorus for Merle Haggard's *Workin' Man Blues.*

"Thought you liked this job." Jimmy nearly jumped out of his skin as Hogan *Boss* Bostick came up behind him. "Guess you're off the train today then."

"What? No! I'm—"

Boss winked at him. Crap! He always fell for the straight line.

"I thought that one mutt was one too many. Now we've got two. Don't know what this railroad is coming to." He walked over to Dilya as if it was the most normal thing in the world and rubbed one of his big hands into Zackie's fur. "Heya. Sorry, I always greet dogs first. They just don't have any understanding about being greeted second. My name's Hogan Bostick. But most folks call me Boss, even though my wife up in the station building is the real boss. Course I've been here longer than most of these trains, so I'm guessin' that makes me the *train* boss at least. Though I'm not making any claims about *Ammonoosuc.* They built her in 1874 and she still be running strong. I'm betting you're that Dilya who has our boy in such a tizzy."

7

"A bet you'd win, Boss," Dilya smiled up at him. He made it easy to do so. She didn't think about why, but she liked the idea that she'd flustered Jimmy.

"That makes you, Zackie, huh?" Boss looked down at her dog. "Never met me a First Dog before."

"I'm sorry to disappoint you, sir. Zackie is no longer First Dog. She's mine now. The First Lady gave her to me when I quit."

"You *quit?*" Jimmy practically shouted.

Boss, a big man with a gray beard worthy of an Arctic explorer, shifted slightly to block Jimmy's sightlines. His smile said he knew exactly what he was doing.

Jimmy circled around him with Merle sticking close by his side. "When? Why? I mean, you're a fixture at the White House since forever. Why would you quit?"

That was a question she wouldn't be answering in front of any third party.

Boss harrumphed at her silence. "I see you two, you four with your dog pals, have some catching up to do. Jimmy Martin, you get the *Abenaki* squared away last night?"

"I did. She's all greased up and good to go."

Boss harrumphed again, this time expressing that he'd have to see about that. "Probably forgot to fill the fuel tank," his whisper was loud enough to be heard halfway up the mountain. "Jimmy Martin, you've got an hour until the first passengers arrive. Think you better go for a walk-and-talk with this girl some before you explode."

"But—"

"I can set the trains for the first run on my own, boy. Just don't dawdle about more'n you have to."

"Okay. Thanks, Boss." She'd expected Jimmy to flop his wavy brown hair forward over his eyes like he used to in high school when he was embarrassed. And though his cheeks flamed red, he continued looking straight at her.

Boss' footsteps crunched away as he walked downslope on the railbed, headed toward a group of sheds at the foot of the track. That must be where they stored the other engines.

The Cog Railway Base Station was a big two-story lodge of a building painted light blue. It sat in a deep valley thick with maples and birches rich with their fall yellows and golds. Up the track, which climbed steeply out of the station, the colors shifted more to orange and red.

"It's good to see you."

"Thanks," she looked back at Jimmy, then down at Merle. "You got a Sheltie, too."

"Uh-huh. I guess I missed Zackie or something." This time he did look away.

Merle studied Zackie. He was definitely interested in meeting another Shetland sheepdog, but Zackie, who Dilya would have bet didn't have a shy bone in her body, still hadn't left Dilya's lap. She herself was having trouble looking at Jimmy.

Enough already.

She shooed Zackie to the ground, then pushed to her feet. Not thinking first, she reached into her pocket and held out the card she'd found. Only after Jimmy took it, as if it might explode, did she realized what she'd done.

"Sorry. I— Val and I found this in an old card catalog at the UN in New York. Trevor and Kimberlee helped me get that far. Miss Watson is in major trouble and she left me this clue. But I don't know how to interpret it. I quit my job because she's in trouble and I've been all over half the country trying to figure out how to help her."

Without the barest glance at it, Jimmy flicked it against his opposite palm with a crisp snap. "So, I'm the last one you come to for help. And all you want is for me to break a code. Thanks but no thanks." He handed back the card.

She hadn't meant it that way. Before she could explain, he called his dog.

"Merle, heel!" There was enough snap in his voice for Merle to look at him in surprise; enough anger to stop Dilya's protest. Merle left his mutual inspection of Zackie and followed Jimmy as he stomped down the hill.

Zackie looked at her in surprise.

Things definitely weren't going the way she'd intended.

They'd walked halfway to the train shed, where a deep rumble said that Boss had another of the engines up and running, before she figured out what to do. It might not work...but it might.

She flicked a hand sign to Zackie. Her dog turned and trotted downslope with absolute trust.

Dilya stood in the chilly morning, alone as usual. It was how she felt most of the time, but this time it hurt.

8

"WANT SOME ADVICE, JIMMY MARTIN?"

"Nope."

Boss offered a thoughtful grunt.

Jimmy ignored him as he eased the next passenger carriage from the storage shed. It was always a fussy job rolling it from its storage rails onto the transfer platform. Once there, he could shift it from the shed line to the main track.

The day they'd upgraded him from shoveling coal for their old steam engine to setting up the trains for the day had been a good one. There existed an order and neatness to it.

The switching layout for the sheds was ingenious. Simple, efficient, and he doubted he'd have ever thought of it. He wanted challenges like that, which would continue to stretch him—without trapping him all day in some office grinding out calcs on...concrete-bearing capacities or beam shear.

He was rolling out the bright blue Number 8 car, when

Boss called out, "Hold up there, Jimmy Martin." Blasted man never called him anything except his full name.

Easier said than done. It took a lot of force to get a car moving, and it took just as much to stop it. By the time he had it stopped, the car's end platform lined up with the edge of the garage slab.

Once he'd locked it in place, Jimmy took a step back and fell on his ass. Yelps of surprise, and the brush of fur racing for safety, punctuated his backward fall onto the hard ground.

He'd left the transfer track lined up—*Oh man!*—with the green car in the next bay over. In another five feet, he'd have run the blue Number 8 off the storage rails and into the dirt, causing who knew how much damage and delay.

He lay there staring up at the carriage that loomed poised to crush him—serious damage.

Two cold wet dog noses poked into his face. He shoved Merle to one side, then looked in surprise to see the other nose was attached to Zackie. A welcoming lick ran up one cheek, across his nose, and into his eye. He'd always liked the dog, or why would he have picked up Merle? But he knew the real answer—because Dilya had a Sheltie. Gods but he was so pathetic.

"C'mon, you two. Give a guy a break." That's when he spotted Boss standing over him with his fists jammed into the pockets of his battered old jacket. "Sorry, Boss."

"Didn't catch on you felt serious about a girl. Might have teased you less about Marsha. Might not have, too. Guess we'll never know."

"I'm not serious about Dilya Stevenson." Mostly because he didn't stand a chance with her.

"Serious enough to not have taken Marsha up on her offer.

I've got eyes, Jimmy Martin. I still can see a beautiful woman when she passes by. Two of them, truth be told. Twice. Two eyes, and two beautiful women both interested in you."

Jimmy shrugged his confusion.

" 'Less I'm mistaken, and I'm not much given to such things, that's her dog come to follow you about."

Jimmy sat up enough to rub both dogs' heads. In response they jumped on his chest and knocked him flat again.

"Aw, cheez."

"I can see that I've got me a few things to teach you before you start driving our engines."

Jimmy wrestled an arm around each Sheltie's neck and they began a tug-of-war game, attempting to free themselves. With them out of his face for the moment, he looked up at Boss carefully.

"First off, *Cheez* is a crap curse. It is neither taking the Lord's name in vain nor is it making a near vile enough comment on Cheez Whiz. Cheese in a can," Boss shuddered. "My ma thought it was the best way to make grilled cheese sandwiches. Our house went through that shit by the case."

Jimmy lost control of Zackie's head and pushed to his feet before the dogs jumped him again. He dug a bakery dog biscuit out of his pocket, snapped it in two and tossed it to the dogs.

For the first time since he was a pup, Merle missed the catch—he was too busy watching Zackie.

"What's the other thing you have to teach me, Boss?"

"That dropping a ten-ton rail car on your chest is a crappy way to avoid talking to a pretty girl."

Jimmy sighed. It was.

9

"LET'S SEE IT."

Dilya shook her head. She'd done a lot of thinking since Jimmy had walked away from her. Moving from the hard steel grate of the train's service walk to a granite bench was more comfortable but far colder on her butt. Six days ago, everything had made sense, now nothing did.

"Dilya."

She shook her head again but she no longer knew for sure what she was saying no to. "Is that what I do? Use my friends? I don't like the way that sounds at all."

Jimmy sat down beside her as the dogs chased circles around the bench before racing off to explore something else. "Even Zackie. I sent her to get you to come back."

"Not why I'm back."

"Why are you?"

Jimmy's shrug revealed that his emotions were as uncertain as her own. She kept her attention on the railroad track. Once out of the station, it crossed a bridge over a narrow rushing river, then began climbing up the steep mountain ridge.

"It wasn't like that. I didn't come to you last. Well, I did, but not on purpose. I was in Tennessee and I knew that Kimberlee had spent a lot of time with Miss Watson, and she was just over in Alabama. She sent me to see Trevor in DC. It turned out Miss Watson had been giving him recipes and also introduced him to a tea librarian."

"A what?"

Dilya shook her head. It would be too confusing to explain fully. "A woman who collects and catalogs teas, drinking ones not golfing ones. She sent me on to the UN where Val and I unraveled what's going on. Miss Watson wasn't the only spy from her years-ago MLIS class."

"Masters in..."

"Library and Information Science. For the last six months, someone has been hunting them down and killing them off. I think they're hunting Miss Watson. She left a clue there for me that Zackie helped find." Now she pulled out the catalog card to stare down at it; to make sure it was still real. "But you're the only person I trust who has a chance of reading it."

"Only person...you trust."

Dilya nodded fiercely but didn't turn away from the track that climbed hundreds of feet before curving to disappear behind a giant maple tree turning a brilliant gold-orange. Her butt had gone past cold and into cryogenic storage; she might never move normally again.

"You don't trust a whole lot of people, do you?"

She shook her head. "Other than the Chef's Club? My stepparents, Emily Beale, Miss Watson, and Frank Adams and his wife." She cast around. There were others she could go to for help, without any questions asked, but trust? That had come hard, since long before watching her parents' assassination in Afghanistan for simply walking over the wrong pass. As if being driven from their home and hovering on the verge of starving to death hadn't already been bad enough.

Jimmy began ticking them off on his fingers. "The Number One Night Stalkers helicopter pilot, an ex-master spy, and the two heads of the former First Family's Secret Service protection details. Man, Dilya. You've got friends like that and you wonder why the rest of us are so scared of you?"

"Scared? Of *me?*"

10

―――――

JIMMY LAUGHED. "YOU SO DON'T GET IT, DO YOU? OKAY, GIVE me the damned card." Dilya was the most overachieving, smartest... Yeah, that whole list of superlatives that had tied his tongue in knots all through high school. And since, he had to admit.

She handed it over and muttered softly to Zackie who had returned with Merle trotting close behind, "I'm not scary, am I?"

Zackie jumped up into her lap and rested her nose on Dilya's shoulder as she hugged the Sheltie.

Did Dilya truly have so few real friends? How did the world appear to her? He looked down at the card. Did he hold a gift? A warning? A clue leading into danger? Someone was murdering a long-ago graduating class of librarians. Miss Watson had to be in her seventies or maybe more.

Miss Watson had talked to Kimberlee almost as often as she talked to Dilya. She'd been feeding recipes and more to Trevor. What in the world was a tea librarian, anyway? Val had always been carrying around some book or other about global politics and was already working at the UN.

What had the old woman done for him? She'd told him *Continue doing what you're doing, young man*. That was it.

"Real helpful, Miss W," he kept the mutter to himself and inspected the card.

It looked like a cipher code. Knowing what little he did of Miss Watson, it wouldn't be an easy one. Unless, of course, it was.

The first line of the card read, *Chef's Club*. "Miss Watson's message wasn't meant for you."

"It wasn't?" Dilya twisted to look at him in surprise.

"Well, not you alone," he pointed to the title.

"I thought—" Then Dilya bit her lower lip hard enough to turn it white.

"You assumed you had to do it on your own. But Miss Watson knew about our Chef's Club. She gave you this, knowing that you'd *have* to come to me last. The others probably could have helped in any order, but it would have been less efficient, going back and forth between us. You simply stumbled on the shortest route: Kimberlee, Trevor, Val, then me."

She tipped her head to indicate a maybe. Her long hair, long with just enough curl to always be in slight disarray, had always fascinated him. It appeared to be as alive as she was, and he'd often convinced himself that he could read her emotions there more easily than on her face.

The code was laid out in fifteen rows, each twenty-six characters long. The twenty-six count was consistent so that had to be a clue. A standard decoding block for the Vigenère code was twenty-six columns wide. That particular cipher had always intrigued him. The most famous unsolved cipher in the world, the fourth panel of the

Kryptos sculpture in the CIA's courtyard, had used a double Vigenère encryption for the first two panels. Dilya's long-ago gift of Elonka Dunin's book about that sculpture had sent him off in a whole new direction of geekdom during high school.

Actually, she'd given him a number of books over the years, everything from cyberwar to geopolitics. War. Conspiracies—*real* ones. It had been enough to convince him that working on a hundred-and-sixty-year-old railroad made more than a modicum of sense.

"What made you think to give me that book about the Kryptos sculpture?"

Dilya's hair fluttered, first one way as Dilya thought back, then the other as she retrieved the memory. "Miss Watson thought that you'd like it."

"I did." He also liked that he hadn't been as ignored by Dilya's mentor as he'd thought. He wondered how many of the various books Dilya had found for him came from Miss Watson and how many from her own insatiable need to understand the world.

Perhaps Miss Watson would expect him to recall that. In which case, he was more assured of the Vigenère cipher. But what were the keywords to unlock it. He tried *Chef's Club* but the first few characters gave him back nonsense. If she hadn't used a standard alphabet, then it would be nearly impossible to decipher.

That didn't fit. She had expected Dilya to find the card and—

O. M. G.

By having Dilya to be the one to give him the code book, Miss Watson had set it up that Dilya would of course bring any code to *him*. But Dilya had said that the was card recent and he'd had the book for years now. Studied it too.

That meant the cipher's key wasn't on the card itself.

The track was getting busy. *Running out of time, Jimmy.* Today's first run included four trains, each made up of one passenger car with a single pusher engine to drive it up the cog railway. The first task of the day was getting them all lined up on the tracks by the base station.

Boss had the first three trains set up already and was easing the fourth, their steam engine, into place. A lot of folks felt nostalgic for steam engines and The Cog always kept one in the collection, even though they were slower and dirtier than the biodiesel ones. It also required a shovelful of coal every three to five seconds for the entire forty-five-minute climb to the peak. He was glad to not be scheduled aboard that today.

Already, early passengers were starting to circulate, madly shooting selfies with the odd-looking engines. Everything was designed to be most comfortable when on the steep grade of the rail line. Here on the near flat of the loading platforms, they looked structurally askew. The steam engine appeared as the oddest of them all. Its boiler tilted at a sharp, nose-down angle, which made it roughly level while climbing up the side of the mountain.

He called Merle over and pointed at the ground by his feet. *Stay* was about the only command he consistently obeyed. Passengers weren't allowed to bring dogs other than Service animals, and workers only under certain circumstances. Thankfully, on the days when he rode as a brakeman, the maintenance team who trekked up the five kilometers of track that climbed over a kilometer in that distance were glad to have Merle along for the ride. On stormy days, the Sheltie hung out with the guys in the shop.

"What would she use as a cipher key other than *Chef's Club?*"

Again, Dilya's hair thought about the question as she first looked down at the dogs lying to either side of their feet and then up at the trains. "It would be something not obvious. Something that a person finding the card would never think of."

Only one way he'd encode it.

Dilya showed promise as a key for the first five characters: *bever. B ever...vigilant?* Or perhaps: *Be very... careful?* Seemed likely. He could almost hear the old woman's voice. But then he was back to gibberish when he tried to repeat her name as the key word, which was how the Vigenère worked. What if the sixth letter was Z for Zackie? Nope. Nor S for Stevenson.

If he assumed that the sixth character was the Y from *very...* It was a slow process as he cranked through the letters of the alphabet in his head without a Vigenère square to refer to. He went one by one but he found it when he reached N. And he tried working the C of *careful* backwards. That matched the keyword A. Reapplying the full name again unraveled the rest of *careful.*

"Dilyana?"

This time her hair whipped aside as she twisted to face him.

"What?" She hanked her hair into a bunch with one hand so he couldn't read it.

Her green eyes, he'd still never seen anything like them, watched him intently. He never knew what to say to those eyes.

"Where did you hear that name?" It sounded as if he might have just fallen out of her tiny group of trust.

"It's the key to this code."

"No one uses that name."

"Sorry. But it's right here on Miss Watson's card for me to find. Or it's not here, but it makes the code work."

Dilya began cursing and pushed to her feet, only to nearly face-plant onto the pavement because Zackie had earlier shifted out of her lap and now lay across her toes.

He managed to catch her arm and she regained her balance. Even through the heavy jacket, he was aware of touching her. Of feeling her whiplike strength.

Which gave him thoughts he'd be better off not thinking. The same ones he'd had since the very first time he'd met her. She was simply the coolest person he'd ever met.

Dilya, Dilyana (?), stepped over Zackie and walked away to glare at one of the engines. Her hair shimmered in the sunlight with how upset she was.

Jimmy glared briefly at the trains himself.

Who was he kidding? He was learning how to be a railroad engineer on one of the oddest trains in the world that boasted only nine engines in the entire system. She raced about the country, uncovering secret clues, and trying to rescue an ex-master spy from a serial librarian murderer. They didn't inhabit the same world, never mind the same league.

Back in DC, there'd been some thin hope while they attended the same high school. Oh sure, the girl who lived in the White House and missed school because she had to zip about on Air Force One, and...him. Mom had been a cop and Dad worked at the mint, as a machinist.

He returned his attention to the code but his eyes wouldn't focus. No one understood how easy it had been to turn down Marsha. It would have been unkind to accept, as experience had taught him that he'd have been thinking of Dilya.

A shadow spread over the card and he looked up to see her standing very close, only separated by where Merle lay across his own feet...something he'd never done before.

She looked at him so intently that he didn't even bother trying to speak. Having her this close was physically painful. This close but still so far.

"No one," her voice barely a whisper, "except my two mothers—the dead one and the one who saved me—ever used that name. It's...private. I can't figure out how Miss Watson even knew it."

She stared at him without blinking until his own eyes watered badly in sympathy.

"I know you won't use it around anyone else. But when it's just us two, it's...," she took a deep breath and let it out in a hard huff. "It's okay."

He was still trying to understand the implications of being granted Dilyana-permission when Boss called out from the window of the *Metallak* biodiesel engine. "It's time, Jimmy Martin."

"Thirty seconds, Boss."

"Not thirty-five," Boss snapped back, showing the first irritation Jimmy had ever heard from him. Not good. *Very* not good.

He was scheduled to have his first full drive to the top today. Instead of being told what to do at every step, he'd be the engineer in charge with Boss there to offer refinements —and to keep him from messing up.

But he'd barely started unraveling the code. He'd bet that if he blinked, Dilya would be gone again from his life. But he couldn't hold her hostage either.

"Here," he held the card for them both to see. "Imagine a square block of letters of twenty-six-by-twenty-six characters. The first row is A-Z. The second one shifts, B-Z with an A on the end to complete the row. Third starts with a C and so on until you have the whole alphabet shifted one letter at a time, row by row."

She nodded.

"Okay. Your name is the key to the cipher. On the left side, go down to the D, that's your row. Go across until you hit the first letter in the message, in this case an E, go up to the top row and your clear text is B. For the second letter, use the second letter of your name, I. Go across the row until you find the second letter of the message, which is M. Go up to the top, the clear text is E. Third letter of your name, Y, paired with the third letter of the message, T, gives you V. When your name runs out, just repeat it. Got it?"

She nodded again.

He could feel Boss' annoyance reaching maximum operating pressure.

"Dilya, wait a sec, okay? Don't go anywhere, please."

She nodded a third time.

He trotted over to Boss to avoid shouting over the heads of boarding passengers, especially when he had no idea what he should say. If he turned down the drive, he'd be labeled unreliable. Uncommitted. If he didn't, Dilya would be gone.

Then he realized that he still held the catalog card of code. Well, she wouldn't be leaving without that. But she'd be furious if he took it with him.

Unless...

11

<hr />

DILYA DID HER BEST TO BE SMALL. SHE WASN'T SURE WHAT Jimmy had said to Boss but the small engine compartment was now quite crowded.

Jimmy sat at the controls of the engine. Boss sat close beside him in the only other seat.

For Dilya he'd propped a crate to rest against the engine cab's rear wall.

"Once we're up on the grade, it'll be a bit like you're tilted back in a seriously slow rocket," Boss winked as she sat. It was warmer than the engine's steel service grate or the ice block of the granite bench which counted as a significant improvement.

The two dogs lay on the only open bit of flooring. The whole locomotive measured only twenty-five feet long and most of that was engine.

"Five more seconds, Boss."

At his nod, Jimmy handed her the card, a pad of paper, and a pen. "Write out the Vigenère square the way I said, A-to-Z, B-to-Z-plus-A, and so on, then you'll be fine." He turned to the controls.

"Okay, Jimmy Martin," Boss' voice shifted to a business-like tone. "You've got a train to run. Now forget about the pretty girl and focus."

"Yes, Boss."

And Dilya watched the change come over Jimmy as well.

In high school he'd been the odd man in the Chef's Club. There'd been the head of the debate club / future politician. The soccer team captain already turning skilled chef. The most popular and smartest girl in school going straight into the diplomatic corps. Herself immersed in White House politics. And Jimmy, the club's geek. He loved computer games yet otherwise kept his sharp mind hidden from most.

With a minimum of fanfare, he'd launched out of high school with so many Running Start credits that he'd graduated from MIT with his Masters in Mechanical Engineering in only three years. Nobody did that.

And yet he was here learning to run a train. Furthermore, looking as if he belonged. A much younger version of Boss.

The train had far fewer controls than she expected. Of course, her frame of reference primarily included the helicopters and airplanes used by the First Family. Even their limousine stocked numerous extra radios for both political calls and security communications, in addition to the controls and readouts for the built-in defensive systems.

Three big levers dominated the console of Jimmy's train. One appeared to be the speed of the motor, another of the locomotive itself. The biggest was bright red and clearly labeled Brake.

"What's your setting on the backstopping clutch?" Boss called out.

Jimmy didn't glance down. "Engaged. She can't roll back."

Boss smacked him on the back of the head, not hard but enough to make Jimmy spin to face him. "You manually and *visually* confirm that every time. It's the most important thing in the entire setup. That's why we've spent so much time and money to design them and put them on every engine and passenger car twenty years back."

"Yes, Boss."

The big man lowered his voice, but Dilya had astute hearing. "Sorry for smacking you in front of your girl, Jimmy Martin, but that's so you never forget. When you're driving on your own, that's the one thing you'll always remember. Like I'm looming right over you every time."

Your girl? Dilya wasn't anyone's girl. Yet Boss had made multiple references to that.

That Dilya who has our boy in such a tizzy.

And Jimmy had been so angry that she'd come to him last. That hadn't been intentional and he'd calmed down once he'd realized that himself.

No, before that. He'd let go of most of his anger *before* he'd come back to her. He did that for her. Because he cared for her?

Definitely a new concept.

Didn't he understand that he belonged in the world in a way she never could?

A slight jar and the engine began rolling forward. She heard the big cog gear in the undercarriage clanking along the track. She twisted enough to look out the back door. There were two lines of steel rail like any other railroad. And in the middle lay a third rail made up of small sideways bars of round steel, like a narrow ladder for very heavy mice placed flat on the railroad ties. The locomotive was driven upward partly by the wheels, but mostly by the cog engaging in the ladder of steel.

As she watched out the back, Dilya saw they were crossing a small river on a high trestle bridge. When they reached the far side, the track tilt changed significantly. Now her shoulder pressed heavily on the rear wall.

The dogs began sliding on the floor. They ended up against the rear wall on the opposite side of the small entry door from her propped crate. Zackie appeared surprised, but Merle simply settled more comfortably ready for a nap. Zackie took her cue from Merle and, after a brief check-in glance with Dilya, did the same.

Dilya placed her own back against the wall and did indeed feel as if she lay in the recliner of Boss' very slow rocket.

She wanted to work on the code, but couldn't stop watching Jimmy. He acted differently when working the train's controls. Every motion was smooth, assured. Per Boss' lesson, he made a point of sweeping his eyes over the few dials and settings at least once a minute.

The awkward kid with the quick sense of humor—one that often caused him trouble in high school—wasn't in evidence.

With a fast-rising but not overloud *klunk-klunk-klunk* the train continued climbing the track. Zackie kept looking up at the strange surroundings, first checking in with her and then with Merle. Dilya wondered quite where Zackie's mind was as she eventually began checking in with Merle first and Dilya second.

During the forty-five-minute climb Dilya barely started the Vigenère diagram she'd need to decode the message. There was too much to see.

She couldn't see the brakeman, riding on the front

platform of the passenger car, at the very head of their little two-vehicle train. Boss told her that he had three duties: first, to keep the passengers entertained and second, to watch for any anomalies on the track. Most importantly, they must be constantly ready to throw the emergency brake.

Whoever the brakeman was, brakewoman for this trip, she kept a constant stream of chatter that engaged Dilya despite the cipher in her lap.

She made jokes about a moose who tended to lurk in the trees close by the track, which never spooked at the train's passage. Dilya saw why when they climbed past a life-size plastic moose watching their passage balefully.

Trees shifted from green and lightly colored to glorious arrays of reds and golds, then finally to bare branches as they climbed into higher and higher climate zones. And while she'd been watching the colors, the trees had become shorter and there were more conifers.

A thick fog shrouded the mountain for most of the ride, but views popped out through brief wind-torn rents as they climbed high above the valley and up on the exposed ridges.

At one point, the brakewoman challenged passengers to, very carefully, try standing. They were presently in the steepest part of the climb. The trees, little more than a few meters tall here, did indeed look to be at an odd angle to the train.

Dilya took the challenge and tried to rise. But she fell back against the rear wall of the cab. She ignored Boss' chuckle. Only when she tucked her feet well under her and leaned so far forward that her head nearly rested on Jimmy's back was she able to stand upright. Zackie attempted to scramble to her feet and became alarmed when she fell sideways against the rear bulkhead. Dilya knelt carefully to soothe her then resumed her *slow rocket* seat for the rest of the journey to the peak.

The break of the timberline happened abruptly, doubly so as the fog boundary launched them into full sunshine. The near-bonsai trees that had been battling the wind and snow for perhaps hundreds of years were gone. Lichen-covered rock, ice-coated grasses, and an expanse of sky so blue that it almost hurt to look at were all that remained.

High above, she could see the building that wrapped around most of the summit.

"See the small monument to the right of the train?" the brakewoman must be talking about the person-tall sign.

The peak lay less than a hundred meters away.

"In 1855 Lizzie Bourne died here, in the dark, at the age of twenty-four—less than a ten-minute walk from the Tip Top House. She hiked up with two family members and they were caught out in an unexpected storm, stopping on this spot because they had no idea they were so close. Lizzie Bourne, the first woman known to have died on Mount Washington."

Dilya stared back at the marker as the train finished the climb.

Where might Miss Watson's grave marker be if Dilya didn't hurry?

She didn't see their final arrival as she focused on drawing a twenty-six-by-twenty-six grid and began writing out the Vigenère decoding square.

12

————————

JIMMY EASED THEM TO A STOP, SET THE HARD BRAKE, AND cycled down the engine to idle. As the brakewoman helped the passengers disembark for their hour at the summit, he ran down the checklist he'd made during training. This was no airplane, so it didn't take long.

Only then did he glance at Boss to see if he'd missed anything.

Boss thumped his shoulder, "Might make a driver of you yet, Jimmy Martin." Then he stepped out the back door and climbed down to the track bed to help with the passengers.

Taking a deep breath, Jimmy turned to face Dilya. But all he saw was her hair.

She was hunched down over the pad he'd given her forty-five minutes ago and scribbling madly. So much for any admiring comments about his driving job.

"It shouldn't have taken that long to decode the message. What went wrong?"

Dilya froze, then raised her head slowly until she looked straight at him. "I, uh..." Dilya being speechless was a new one on him.

She handed him the pad.

It had less than half of the decoding square, and none of the message done.

He looked back at Dilya. The sun streaming into the cab lit her face brightly. Despite her tan-dark complexion, her cheeks looked distinctly red.

Jimmy couldn't help laughing and she offered one of her rare smiles in return.

"There was so much to see. Out the window and how you—" again her words stumbled to a halt.

To rescue her, he snapped a leash on Merle. "Come on. We've got a couple minutes before we head back down. We can at least stretch our legs. Let the dogs lift a leg. Where's Zackie's leash?"

"She doesn't need one." Dilya tapped her left thigh and Zackie shifted to stand close beside her.

"Merle is a hazard. I've tried, but progress is slow." He opened the door and let Merle lead them outside. A sharp chill and a strong wind replaced the snug warmth of the cabin. A glance back at the thermometer showed that they'd moved from fifty-three degrees to twenty-one by climbing the mountain. And he'd guess that the wind was twenty gusting thirty.

"I could help you with him," Dilya said. "It only takes time and knowing how to train them."

He liked the image...until he had a nasty thought. It took a deep breath before he could say it without the hurt racing out from his insides to blast her. "How many minutes after you decode that message will you be here?"

"Not many, I guess." She glanced downslope, as if wishing she hadn't come up the mountain at all. "Otherwise I'll be putting up a marker for Miss Watson's like Lizzie Bourne's."

Jimmy glanced at the distant white marker. He'd never given it a thought except for pitying the woman who'd died most of two centuries ago. Dilya's comment left him feeling foolish. Again, he drove a train five whole kilometers and Dilya held someone's life in her hands.

He turned to the railing at the edge of the train platform, the wind ripping tears from his eyes. Jimmy wasn't weeping, but the wind made it feel as if he was.

All of the passengers had climbed off the opposite side. A few brave souls would circle the top, or walk out on the viewing platform. Most hit the ten-below wind chill and scuttled into the combined museum-gift shop-cafeteria to await their descent time.

He looked at the railing. Icicles trailed all along the outside face of the rail. It wasn't the downwind side. Water molecules being blown into the rail's wind shadow and eventually freezing there didn't form these. Atop Mount Washington, the moisture hit the front of the rail and froze there instantly, building sideways icicles that grew *into* the wind.

Time. There was never enough time around Dilya. He wanted to freeze this moment in place, before Dilya raced off.

She tried to pull out the card, but it slapped and snapped in the chill wind and she shoved it back into her pocket before the wind took it from her.

"Jimmy Martin," Boss bellowed against the wind as he strode up to them. He'd zipped his vest, but his heavy jacket still hung open.

Jimmy had zipped his up tight enough to choke.

"Think you should skip this return. Show your lady friend the sights. Might be the last chance of the season. Storm's coming in and might be closing the top early this season," he nodded toward the northwest where clouds were building in the distance. "I'll be back to the top with another load of tourists in an hour and a half. You can run that descent with me."

Boss didn't wait for an answer, merely walked to the engine and climbed aboard.

Jimmy wanted to kiss the old man.

13

DILYA FOLLOWED JIMMY OVER THE ICY STONE PATHS, AND PAST the heavy rock walls of the TipTop House. It was closed, but had been there as a hostel back in the time of Lizzie Bourne.

Would she be this close to the finish and fail as Lizzie had so long ago? Would Dilya forever regret the loss of rescue time from taking this brief break?

Yet when Jimmy held her gloved hand with his to steady her at the very summit, she couldn't regret the moment. In every direction the land lay below them. Bare peaks, rivers snaking along forested valleys, and the wind buffeting them like it embodied an eternal force that would never be beaten. It ruffled the Shelties' thick fur in every direction until they both looked like dust mops.

By the time they had circled the top and seen every view, she couldn't stop shivering and didn't care. They were laughing as they ducked into the building where all the other train passengers had long since taken refuge.

"See how the ramp goes up from the doors to the main level?"

Dilya nodded as they ascended along with all of the others moving up and down the level.

"It keeps the heat in. Heat rises. This ramp climbs over a story, so as people come in and out the doors, the warm air stays up there in the main part of the building. Energy conservation through design."

She stopped in the middle of the ramp, causing a minor traffic jam. The two of them didn't take up much room, but the two dogs swirling about their legs consistuted a hazard. Jimmy saw things she didn't. How different a world did he see? It had purpose and structure in ways she'd never imagined.

Thinking nothing of it, he led her the rest of the way up the ramp. The upper level was a wide-open area with heavy beams, bright wood, and a view that curved around one whole side of the summit.

She bought postcards at the gift shop while Jimmy went to the cafeteria.

In minutes they were sitting by one of the windows, its outside edges rimmed with ice, but the view remained spectacular. He handed her a chili dog and a hot chocolate. She hadn't stopped for breakfast this morning, so even a mid-morning chili dog looked delicious.

"Let's see it." Jimmy knew that the delay must be eating at her. She handed over pad, pen, and finally the catalog card. He continued filling out the Vigenère square, once he thawed out the pen enough to make it work. With nothing to do for the moment, she looked at the cheerful crowds gathered along the wooden tables. For a tourist place, it was surprisingly cozy. The room resonated with the energized chatter of the tourists invigorated by their outing and now comfortably warm inside. And the hot chocolate warming her from the inside certainly helped.

It was so different from the White House. There was a constant buzz there, but it was usually serious except when it tipped over into intense. Silence only descended in the late hours when the desperation to get one more thing done that day settled over those who remained. Everything here felt lighter, safer.

Didn't they know how dangerous the world was? No, nor did they need to. There were brief moments when she wished she didn't either. Being a realist, not a pessimist, it still wouldn't hurt her to focus on the positive more. On simply appreciating the moment.

She jotted out the postcards, seeking to be both brief and upbeat. A panoramic photo of Mount Washington to each of the Chef's Club, a quick Hello to Emily in Montana, and a Thank You to the First Lady. Dilya signed that one with an outline of a pawprint.

"Okay," Jimmy handed her back the catalog card. "Start reading off the letters and say the letter count of each one so that we don't get lost."

"One, E," she started. "Two, M. Three, T. Four..." They worked their way through the entire message. Every multiple of seven, she reminded him to start the cipher code over to keep them in sync. "Eight, restarting my name..."

When she finished, Jimmy didn't give her the message right away. She looked over to see that he'd laid it out in neat rows, exactly matching the layout on the catalog card.

"I'm just checking to see if there's a second level of encoding."

"A second level?"

"Sure," Jimmy didn't look up. "For example, does the first letter of each line spell out an additional message? It doesn't. Is there a hidden word search?" He began running the pen close above the page along different lines and diagonals. But kept shaking his head. "If there is, I'm not seeing anything else." He then went through the decryption, marking quick slashes between each word. "Sometimes there's an encoding for a space, most commonly an X, but Miss Watson hadn't done that. It's like a run-on word with no breaks or punctuation." He finished and pushed it across the wood table to her.

"What's it say?"

"Uh," then Jimmy laughed. "I didn't actually read it. Not for content." He leaned forward until their heads almost touched to read it upside down. Then jolted and turned to look out the window at the sound of a steam whistle.

Dilya followed where he was looking. At peak capacity, like today, the Mount Washington Cog Railway sent four trains to the top every forty-five minutes. Since their arrival, a second group had come. It left again, taking the first passengers down, while she and Jimmy were looking at all the sights. Now another set of trains were pulling into the summit station.

Jimmy looked at his watch. "Wow! That seemed fast. We've got to go. There's a post office over there, you can mail your postcards. Hurry though." And he raced away with Merle at his heels.

In any group, Dilya knew that others felt compelled to keep up with her. Moving slowly simply wasn't in her nature. But Jimmy left her a little breathless. She hustled over to the postmaster, bought stamps, and slid her postcards into the small red and blue steel mailbox. A small sign assured her that they'd be franked for the Top of Mount Washington Post Office.

She and Zackie hurried down the ramp. Jimmy waved from the cab of *Metallak*, the white locomotive they'd ridden to the top. They boarded as the last of the passengers headed down the mountain took their seats.

They were halfway down the mountain before she remembered the message in her pocket and pulled it out to read. By the end of it, she understood even less than she did before. There was no cell signal up here. She'd have to wait for the bottom to research the meaning.

14

DESCENDING THE MOUNTAIN WAS A FAR RISKIER OPERATION than climbing it and Jimmy knew he'd messed it up the whole way down.

On the ascent, the clutch on the cogs were set so that they literally couldn't slide backward. Like a one-way ratchet, they could climb but the safety mechanism wouldn't let the axle spin in the wrong direction.

To descend, that clutch had to be disengaged. Gravity made the engine wanted to race down the steep grade. That was especially true with a massive carriage filled with a hundred people—who weighed eight or ten tons on their own—pushing against his engine from the uphill side. Only by careful tending to the throttle on his part, and the passenger car's brake on the brakeman's part, had they done it safely.

He didn't even dare to pause long enough to unzip his jacket. He was sweating by the time they returned to the Base Station, and it wasn't only because of the jacket.

"That, Jimmy, was a right fine piece of driving." It was the first time Boss had ever used less than his full name.

The sag of relief at being done kept him from showing his pleasure.

"When was the last time you took a day off?"

Jimmy shrugged. He didn't have anywhere else to be. On his days off, he generally came in to learn what he could.

"Thought as much." Boss winked and nodded toward the back of the cab. "Take a couple days." Then he was gone.

Dilya bent over her phone, looking something up. Her hair covered her in a shroud.

Too drained to do more than watch her, he remained where he sat.

The hair shifted as she looked from the phone in her hand to the message pad resting on her thigh. Back and forth twice more as if to confirm. Then she pushed to her feet and he knew that in seconds she'd be gone.

"Dilya," his voice sounded dry and cracked as an old man's. Way to impress her.

She brushed her hair aside to look at him.

"You headed out?"

She nodded.

"Need some company?"

She tipped her head, so that her hair shimmered down over one shoulder almost to her elbow as she thought about it.

"I've got some time coming. If there's any way I can help..." Who was he kidding? Since when did Dilya Stevenson need anyone's help. Yet, she had. She'd come to each of the Chef's Club, *including* him. How new was that for her?

"Really?" Her voice sounded small, even in the confines of the quiet steel cab of the locomotive.

"Really."

"I have to get to DC, by tonight."

DC? Well, Dad had been bugging him to come down for a visit. Then he smiled at her.

"Your car or mine?"

When she threw her arms around his neck, Jimmy knew that, for once, he'd done absolutely the right thing.

PART FIVE

THE TWO-DOG SOLUTION

1

Dilya Stevenson sent two text messages, then passed out in the passenger's seat before he'd even pulled out of the parking lot of The Cog Railway.

Jimmy glanced in the rearview mirror at the trains that carried thousands of tourists to the top of Mount Washington. It was the highest peak in the Northeast and, after four months working there, he felt as if he was leaving something important behind.

He hadn't quit his job here.

Yet, still in the parking lot in the middle of New Hampshire, a piece of him had gone missing. There was a friendly pace here wholly different from his childhood in Washington, DC or his last few years at MIT earning his Masters in Mechanical Engineering. He'd miss the pace and he'd miss the people.

But another part of him now lay sleeping in the passenger seat.

At the first curve, the railway, the Marshfield Base Station lodge, and his comfortable life, all disappeared behind the golden birch and red-orange maple trees of the chill September day. He'd made a place for himself here, learning about the trains and how to drive them. Some day he hoped to help design them.

As he followed the narrow two-lane road twisting through the trees down to the barely larger two-lane *highway* in the valley, he could only hope he'd be back.

On the surface, he was taking a few days off to drive a friend to Washington, DC in her Mini Cooper car and visit Dad.

But with Dilya Stevenson, futures were never so straightforward. Things happened fast when she was around. Yesterday, out of the blue, she'd said she was coming to see him in northern New Hampshire. She'd arrived a bare four hours ago and now he was racing south in a desperate attempt to save her mentor from some killer who'd been hunting the ex-master-spy Miss Watson.

He looked again in the rearview mirror, hoping for one last glimpse of the life he'd been enjoying so much.

Instead, he saw the noses of their two dogs glaring at him from the back seat. The two Shetland Sheepdogs, her Zackie and his Merle, were used to riding in the front seat of their respective vehicles, the seat Dilya slept in.

He shook his head at them and swore he heard the mutual dog sighs before they turned once more to watch out the side windows.

Dilya had said she'd slept only a few hours in the last six days and the way she'd collapsed, he believed her. She'd raced all over the East, from Alabama to DC and the UN in New York, chasing clues to help her save Miss Watson.

It had taken the help of every member of their old high school group, the Chef's Club, to unravel what was happening. The four of them had come together junior year, putatively to visit different restaurant kitchens and learn from the chefs. Because it was Washington, DC, it had quickly become lessons in various global cultures to be learned from Thai, Ethiopian, Japanese, and other chefs.

Then they'd talked their way into the White House kitchen and met Dilya. She'd always been a mystery at school, that girl who worked as the First Nanny and First Dog Sitter. Who actually *lived* in the White House for crying out loud.

She'd kept to herself, making her easy to miss...for most kids. To him she'd stood out as bright as a lighthouse beacon. The top of almost every class, yet he'd seen her intentionally screw up on exams. Never by much. Just enough to stay off the valedictorian radar. That she'd left to Val, the founder of the Chef's Club. The other three of them had vied valiantly for salutatorian—which Kimberlee had snagged, Dilya remaining quietly and carefully in their slipstream.

But at that first meeting in the White House kitchen, they'd inducted her into the club. And she'd transformed it into a think tank for the future because that's the kind of thing she did...well, without thinking. Jimmy didn't know if she was a genius, but she was brilliant in so many ways that it didn't matter.

At the base of the mountain, the road swung wide around the Mount Washington Resort in Bretton Woods. It was an odd spot for major international conferences, but they held a number of them here despite its remoteness from any decent airport. Perhaps the attraction was the isolation itself. Other than Mount Washington, the only activities were hiking, fishing, and skiing. And leaf peeping.

He waited at the train tracks as the *Mountaineer,* a Conway Scenic Railway train, rolled through to their endpoint station a hundred meters farther on. Slowing to a crawl, someone opened one of the side doors.

And there was Marsha, looking out at him.

She'd been mounting a major campaign to date him ever since he'd arrived in the area. She was tall and beautiful, yet he'd avoided her. And now that Dilya slept in the seat beside him, he finally knew why.

Marsha watched him as she slowly shifted through his field of vision.

No sassy wink. No air-hip check with a radiant smile. Just...thinking. Her attention briefly slid to Dilya, who he'd arranged to sleep on Marsha's couch for a few hours last night after she'd arrived exhausted in the wrong town—at the other end of the *Mountaineer's* route.

Then Marsha nodded thoughtfully and sent him a friendly salute, one that might have been a goodbye, before disappearing around the final curve. It tempted him to pull in and ask her what that meant. He liked Marsha. He simply hadn't wanted to date her.

But there wasn't time.

If the secret code that Dilya had found hidden at the UN and needed him to decipher was accurate, then Miss Watson was in terrible danger and needed help by tomorrow afternoon at the latest. Dilya hadn't explained why.

DC lay nine hours away. It was already noon.

As soon as Marsha's train cleared the tracks, he turned onto the highway and punched south.

2

————————

HE MANAGED TO ROUSE HER WHEN HE STOPPED AT MUNROE'S in Twin Mountain. He'd phoned ahead and they'd made him two mushroom-Swiss burgers that they were both partial to—he hoped she still was. And two bare burgers, uncooked, for the dogs.

She ate it, took a sip of her root beer, and passed out again with no other clear indication that she'd actually been conscious for it.

He picked up I-93 South and aimed for DC.

He set the cruise control to free up his attention. Quickly bored by the highway, the two dogs curled up for a nap together. At least they got along.

Then he tried to think about the code Dilya had brought him. He didn't have much luck. Every time he tried to focus on it, he kept remembering that she'd driven all of the way from New York to New Hampshire to ask for *his* help. And that he'd been kind of a shit about it.

Dilya Stevenson had always flummoxed him. He was a DC local boy who'd stumbled into one of the city's most elite schools because his family happened to live a block away. When the district had tried to palm him off on Metro High, his mom had stalked into the main office with his test scores clenched in her fist. She'd been a DC cop, the kind that no one in their right mind would ever mess with.

Soon after, close by Washington Metropolitan High School, she'd run into someone *not* in her right mind. He still couldn't stand to venture into the neighborhood where Mom and her partner were gunned down during a *domestic*.

In contrast, Dilya had been this White House goddess. He'd lost count of how many times they'd pulled her out of class because the First Family was flying halfway around the world and needed her as First Nanny.

Exotic—with tan-dark skin, ruffled black hair that wafted about her shoulders, and the greenest eyes on the planet—he'd rarely spoken coherently in her presence. When the club was together, he pretended he was talking to the others and could function like he was at least partly human. On his own with her? Well, he'd proven today how crap he was at that.

Yet she'd hugged him fiercely when he'd asked if she wanted company on her race to DC. That was something he'd *never* forget. Nor how she'd let him lead her by the hand through the icy battering wind atop Mount Washington. Or while sitting over hot cocoa as he'd deciphered her coded message from Miss Watson. And...

Yeah.

He'd figured that once they were in the car, they'd discuss the message's contents. But she'd collapsed with exhaustion.

The process of decryption hadn't required him to read the message, instead he'd been solely focused on a letter-by-letter analysis and that the letters were forming clear text words.

He recalled most of it. Some made sense, some didn't.

After warning her to *Be very careful* in the first line, Miss Watson had turned around with a counterintuitive instruction. *Use ID prominently. Use my name. Visit as many head librarians as possible in one half day: LOC, Folger, Ink, Mint, NPM...* The list was long. *CIA last. Then meet me at SLA tradeshow 1pm.*

He'd recognized the LOC as the Library of Congress like any DC kid would. Folger? Was that the Shakespeare one? NPM might be the National Postal Museum. He recognized less than half of the others, though he certainly recognized the CIA. And he had the nasty feeling that if Dilya and Miss Watson were involved that it wasn't the Culinary Institute of America they were talking about.

And what was the SLA tradeshow? Was that like a show about spying tradecraft? If so, he *definitely* didn't want to know about that.

Into the deep end. Was he ready for that?

He checked on his passengers, all still asleep.

Dilya Stevenson. Asleep beside him. Even in a car zipping south, it was an unexpected gift. Yeah, if she was involved, he was on board wherever it led them. He tried not to think about that, but it was a long quiet drive.

3

———

DILYA WOKE TO A CRICK IN HER NECK THE LIKES OF WHICH made her afraid to move. The least shift of position and her head might fall off. She eased upright with the greatest of care and discovered that while her head might remain attached, she might be happier if it hadn't. Shooting pangs of overstretched muscles released only a tiny bit at a time.

Car seat.

She didn't recognize it at first. But... Oh! She'd bought this car five days ago in Tennessee. Or had it been Kentucky? South Carolina. Four days. She rubbed at her eyes. Four days of chasing—

Dilya jolted upright.

Darkness. Night.

She sat in her car's passenger seat. Parked in some rest area.

Zackie offered a half-awake whine from the back seat. Moments later, two dog heads popped forward between the seats. Her own Sheltie and Merle, who belonged to—

Slumped in the driver's seat like someone had shot him lay Jimmy Martin. He'd...

Her brain finally came fully online. He'd agreed to help her drive back to DC.

She reached out a tentative hand to touch his. It was warm, though he didn't stir. A finger slipped around his wrist and she found his pulse. Steady and solid. She released a breath she didn't realize she'd been holding.

Alive. Sleeping. Not dead. That was good.

Why had he stopped here of all places? Not that she knew where it was. Out the window, all she saw was a couple of lights shining on empty sidewalks, a dumpster, and the inevitable concrete block bathrooms trying to pretend that they didn't look like exactly what they were.

"Jimmy?"

When he didn't wake, she shook his shoulder a little. His head, which had managed to rest at an uneasy equilibrium against the seat's headrest, slipped to the side and hit the window with an audible *Thunk!*

"Ow! What? Where are we?"

"I'd hoped that you knew that."

Jimmy blinked out the window, but didn't come fully awake until Merle licked his face. "Oh. I didn't mean to fall asleep."

"Why didn't you wake me? We could have switched."

"Uh, you needed the sleep. I figured that I'd close my eyes for a minute and dredge up some reserves. Sorry. Guess I didn't have any. Didn't sleep much last night." His grimace said *not at all.* Had that been because of her pending arrival? Why would he have been worried about that?

The whines from the back seat were escalating.

"Dog walk area behind us," he hooked a thumb over his shoulder. "I've got it."

He opened his door and the dogs both zoomed over his lap, squeezing between his chest and the steering wheel.

Hard slaps to his face with their thick tails as they wriggled by, left him spluttering and wiping at his face.

Dilya laughed aloud.

"That's a sound I don't hear much from you." He turned to her.

"I laugh plenty."

"Not that I've ever heard." He slid out of the car and called to the dogs, waving them toward the assigned grassy area.

Sure she laughed. Okay, maybe not often, but she was sure she had. Of course, there'd not been much to laugh about since her parents' murder in the Hindu Kush mountains when she was nine. Her life was good, but laughter? Her stepdad Archie frequently offered a low chuckle, but stepmom Kee, a top military sniper, not so much.

Dilya clambered out of the car to stretch the last of the kinks out of her body. Jimmy's laugh carried easily from the mostly empty rest area. Since she'd woken, two cars had arrived and one left, but at this hour no one seemed hurried.

This hour? She checked her phone. Midnight? After sleeping twelve straight hours in the car, no wonder her neck felt the way it did. The real problem was that car sleep was like airplane sleep, at best a breakeven proposition but never truly restful.

She tried, but her head wouldn't be turning comfortably to the left for hours to come.

They should have been in DC by nine, or ten with bad traffic. A quick check on her map app said they were an hour out.

Jimmy must have stopped three or four hours ago and fallen asleep once he'd parked. That meant he'd driven the whole way without any complaint, simply to allow her to catch up on her sleep.

She tried to see him in the dark but caught no more than a silhouette racing back and forth on the rest area lawn, chased by a pair of happily yipping Shelties.

Jimmy had a good laugh that carried easily across to her. She remembered that from high school too. And he used it often and easily. His quick mind turned everything into a game. He'd even made the President laugh when Dilya had introduced the members of the Chef's Club to him.

A gift. It was some kind of a gift that she didn't have. People liked her well enough—at least the ones she cared about. But none shared laughter with her.

Dilya took over the driving for the last leg.

In minutes, despite his exercise with the dogs, he'd once again fallen asleep. She wondered if she should warn him about the painful crick he'd have if he kept sleeping like that.

Instead, she focused on getting them into DC.

There they could both sleep for a few hours before she had to start on Miss Watson's totally mad task.

4

———

"Morning, Dilya. Whose car?"

Dilya blinked at Linda and her mutt Thor. "Uh, mine. What are you doing working the graveyard shift on the fence?" Their usual shift was daytime inside the White House itself, not at the outer gate.

Linda smiled as Thor sniffed around the tires and under her car. She rolled down the back window enough for Zackie and Merle to peer down at him. Thor didn't look like much, but Dilya knew that he and Linda had saved a lot of lives during an attack on the White House.

Thor was on duty and ignored the two Shelties past a simple glance and a quick sniff to make sure they wouldn't explode any time soon.

"Filling in for Juanita. She's off at a wedding shower."

"She's getting married?" How had Dilya missed that?

"A cousin. Who's sleeping beauty over there?" Linda ducked down to peer across at Jimmy, who still slept.

"Jimmy Martin. You might remember him from my Chef's Club."

"I do. I'll still need his ID and yours."

She nudged Jimmy awake enough to hand over his wallet. He leaned his head on the window and headed once more toward sleep.

Then he jolted upright. "Cheez! We're at the White House?"

"Oh, very observant. Got yourself a winner there, Dilya," Linda laughed. "You two stay where you are." She handed their IDs off to a second guard who had stayed in the small hut but kept a sharp eye on them. Linda walked Thor around the car, sniffing at every corner. The Shelties followed Thor from window to window, trampling on Jimmy whenever necessary. Dilya was spared as she'd preemptively blocked them by holding onto the steering wheel with her right hand, elbow out.

"Hey, cut that out, you two." They ignored Jimmy's protests.

"Grab hold of Merle."

At her instruction, he wrapped his arms around his dog. Dilya whispered "*Fuirich*" to Zackie, who instantly settled.

Jimmy blinked in surprise, then smiled. "I forgot that Zackie speaks Scottish Gaelic."

"What does Merle speak?"

"Dog. And not very fluently. Think he'd respond to Gaelic?"

At Linda's signal by the rear of the car, Dilya popped the hatchback. Thor took a sniff as the two Shelties strained to watch him, then Linda swung it closed.

"It's the training, not the language."

"Well, starting from near zero, Gaelic sounds like fun."

Dilya agreed that it could be. Except it would take far more than the day or so they were both in DC.

Linda chatted for a moment with the hut guard, then returned to the car. "You armed?"

Dilya shook her fighting knife loose from its wrist sheath and held it out. "Only my usual."

Linda nodded and waved it away and looked at Jimmy. "You?"

"Uh. After Dilya, this is going to look kinda stupid." He pulled out a Leatherman Multi-Tool.

Linda shook her head. "I'm sorry. You don't have the clearance to carry that inside the White House Grounds."

"How about if I carry it for him?"

"It can't ever be in his possession inside the grounds. When not on your person, it must remain locked in your registered weapons' safe. If he's found so much as cutting an apple with it, that would be bad."

"I'll make sure." Dilya took it and slipped it into her pocket.

"But—"

"Leave it, Jimmy. It took over a year for me to get clearance in the White House and another year to qualify for Yankee White, meaning I can be armed around the President. Even if he isn't home right now."

They parked the car on West Executive Drive and headed for the West Lobby entrance.

5

"AND YOU WONDER WHY YOU SCARE EVERYBODY?" JIMMY asked Dilya as she led them deep into the White House. After the third turn, he wondered if he'd be able to find his own way out. Dilya then led him through about twenty more and a couple of staircases,.

"No, but I sort of like being scary. Mom can be incredibly scary."

"Only because she's the top sniper in the country and works on the national Hostage Rescue Team."

"Exactly," Dilya sounded pleased. They descended two more flights, went up another, and back down the prior one. They ended up in a basement corridor somewhere deep in the White House. Tables and chairs were stacked along one side. A lump of rolled-up carpet lay on the other. In front of them, a metal door stood ajar.

"Mechanical 043. What's in here?"

Dilya pushed the door open slowly but stayed at the threshold, looking in. "Nothing," in a voice so sad it almost made *him* want to cry.

"This is where she...?"

Dilya nodded.

Miss Watson's office. He'd never been in here. It looked like a concrete cube with a couple of empty bookcases.

Zackie slid between them into the room with Merle following. They circled the room sniffing, and her dog looked almost as sad as Dilya.

He waited, but she didn't move.

When he couldn't stand it anymore, he slapped his thigh to call the dogs back into the corridor. Then he swung the door closed and wrapped an arm around Dilya's shoulders. She didn't resist as he turned her away.

Except...he had no idea where he was beyond a basement deep in the White House.

Barely raising her finger from where her hands hung lax by her hips, Dilya pointed toward the staircase they'd descended. Through far fewer turns and only two sets of staircases, they reached a simple white door. She swung it open and stepped in.

Now he was the one frozen at the threshold. In all the trips that the Chef's Club had made to the White House after Dilya joined them, none of them had ever seen her bedroom. They'd talked about it once when she missed a meeting, but how she lived had remained a mystery.

The room was smaller than his dorm room at MIT. A desk, dresser, and a wide closet. A small bathroom, a bookcase, and a twin bed. No posters on the wall. No TV or stereo. The only thing in the room that wasn't white or wood was the bed quilt. It looked like a mad, multi-colored pointed star made up of rings of diamond shapes ranging across the color spectrum in decreasing wavelengths from violet to deepest red, with a background of the midnight sky.

"I thought you quit. Why are we here?"

"This is home. More than with my stepparents. They were still overseas on assignment when I came to the US. Geneviève insisted I live here. I was ten, though they thought I was thirteen. The only one who knows I quit is Anne. I doubt she'd tell anyone other than her husband. I haven't even told Frank and Beat."

Jimmy tried to remember how to breathe. She referred to the former and present First Ladies by their first names. And, by her descriptions Frank and Beat were two of the scariest people on the planet...heck, in the solar system. They were the respective heads of the protection details for the former President and First Lady.

Dilya crossed to a small safe and locked his Leatherman tool inside next to the big knife he'd seen the first time he'd met her in the White House kitchen. She'd faced down the head chef—not at knife point, but faced him down all the same. The main thing Jimmy recalled was how vicious the black-anodized steel had looked in her grasp and the absolute surety of how she'd handled it.

That was the moment he'd fallen for her. He knew, in that instant, that he'd never meet anyone else like her. Back then, Jimmy had barely managed to gasp out *Super cool*. He had yet to decide if they were the dumbest first words ever said to a girl, but they'd been absolutely true. How little he'd known of the vast extent of Dilya's super wicked über-coolness that was revealed over the next two days alone.

There was very little of her in the room. Four pictures, no more. A tall blonde in a flight suit standing in front of a lethal looking helicopter. Next to it, one of her stepmom sprawled on the ground, sighting along a sniper rifle nearly as long as she was. Dilya and her stepparents on a big sailboat. And a copy of the one Chef's Club photo they'd ever taken, the five of them grinning like idiots in Pauley's Kitchen, one of the city's best restaurants.

"I have that photo too." He pulled out his wallet. It was crumpled, with one end curled by the bend of the wallet and a big crease across the middle. It was the only one he carried a physical copy of other than his parents. He held it next to the one on Dilya's dresser as if to prove their connection, at least to himself.

Dilya said as little as usual but nodded her approval, as if it meant something to her as well. He tucked it away carefully. The group had always been important, but Dilya's image was the reason he still carried it three years after they'd gone their separate ways to college.

"We can get a couple hours sleep."

"Uh…" He eyed the bed. The few hours he'd managed in the car hadn't begun to address the deficit and it was now two a.m.. He looked again. It was still only a twin, exactly as it had been when he'd first seen it a minute ago. The only other surface in the room big enough to sleep on was the floor.

She kicked off her shoes and shed her jacket. "If they can do it, so can we."

Zackie and Merle had doggie piled together into the dog bed by the head of Dilya's twin. Close enough that she could reach out and pet the dog without even raising her head from the pillow.

"I, uh…" He caught her smiling at him. "Sorry, that constitutes the most coherent statement I can make about that offer."

"All I was suggesting is sleep. If I suggested more, how tongue-tied would you become?"

"Super wicked über-tongue-tied."

She laughed. It was a bright sound that seemed to fill the room.

He felt the smile pulling at his own lips.

Then she sobered abruptly. "That first day in the kitchen? It was the first compliment I ever had from anyone in high school."

"Anyone?"

"I don't think a single teacher ever did either. No one noticed me outside of Chef's Club."

"Sure they did. They were simply too scared to talk to you."

Dilya watched him with those green eyes until he couldn't turn away. "Are you too scared?"

"Might be." But he shed his shoes and jacket and let her lead him to her bed.

His face ended up in her hair on the pillow. She smelled of the mountaintop cold they'd found this morning in New Hampshire, and the warmth of the woman. Under the thick quilt, he dared greatly and tucked an arm around her waist.

How could something so slender be a part of someone so strong?

Where did that strength come from? So much more than he possessed himself.

Her sense of absolute surety could account for it.

Or perhaps it was raw nervous energy.

Already half asleep, she pressed back against his chest, sighed once, and was out.

He figured he was about to become a cliché and lie awake the rest of the night, morning, whatever, because it would be impossible to sleep with her in his arms.

That thought lasted him less than three minutes.

6

"WHAT ARE WE DOING HERE?" JIMMY'S VOICE HELD A DISTINCT tone of panic.

"I'm asking to meet the head of the Library of Congress."

"I know that. I get that we're laying down some kind of trail. But now I'm thinking about who's going to be following that trail and find us."

It was the *we* and *us* that was causing her trouble this morning—in many ways.

She'd never woken in a man's arms before. She hadn't even managed a first kiss until college. And a tryst with a boy had never happened. There'd been as big a social bubble around her there as there'd been in high school—without the Chef's Club to offer any respite.

Returning to her duties at the White House directly after classes hadn't helped either. The nights she stayed with her adoptive mom and dad offered an almost comic change. They all loved each other desperately, as their lives had more than once depended on each other. However, her parents' natural protectiveness meant she could descend into the womb of family, but no boy brought into that circle would stand a chance, so she never tried.

Waking up in Jimmy's arms, even fully clothed? She definitely wanted to try that again under other circumstances.

"I thought you'd be visiting your dad." She hadn't expected Jimmy to insist he was coming with her.

"Ha!" His sarcasm was all he offered in reply. He knew that she didn't need his protection. If anything, it would be the other way around. She was the one trained by the Secret Service in self-defense and situational awareness.

"Which means...what?"

"I'm here for *you*, Dilya."

She wished she had time to think about that, but the head librarian had come out to the main floor of the Main Reading Room. They'd been waiting at the circular central desk beneath the library's magnificent dome. When the library doors opened, they'd been first through the door. Only a few of the most eager researchers and tourists had arrived with them and were now finding places at the tiers of circular reading tables.

There were so many things to show Jimmy here: a Gutenberg Bible, Thomas Jefferson's personal library, the rough draft of the Declaration of Independence displayed on the second floor with Adams and Franklin's edits. But there wasn't time. Not with the long list of libraries Miss Watson had left her. Left *them?*

To bring their dogs inside, Zackie wore her *Service Dog* vest and Merle a *Service Dog in Training* one she'd kept from Zackie's early days. Merle fidgeted with excitement.

"Miss Stevenson," the librarian greeted her. He was a tall, hefty man with a broad smile and a deep voice wholly unbefitting her image of a librarian. "To what do I owe the pleasure of this visit?" His glance down at the White House badge she'd left dangling around her neck stated the only reason he'd agreed to see her.

"I'm seeking any information you might have about Miss Watson."

"Miss Watson?" He attempted to look bland, but he lowered his voice and quickly scanned the room. No one appeared to be paying them any mind.

"Yes." Dilya was guessing at the intent of Miss Watson's message and therefore kept her voice normal. "Miss Watson went missing approximately seven days ago and I'm trying to find her. Do you have any information about that?"

"Missing?" his voice now little more than a whisper.

"Yes."

No longer able to hide his distress, he shook his head.

She thanked him and turned to go.

"Miss Stevenson?"

Dilya turned to face him.

"That is a name I would not bandy about so lightly. Where did you hear it?"

"She's been my mentor for the last eight years. I'm following her instructions."

To that, he had no answer as she turned and left him riveted in place.

7

Jimmy's head was soon spinning.

Next they'd visited the Law Library of Congress in the James Madison Memorial Building. The reading room there was thoroughly modern, with none of the grandeur of the Main Reading Room next door. It didn't need it. It was the access point to a complete printed set of every document generated by the United States Supreme Court and that was grandeur enough.

The map collection in the basement was staggering. He could happily get lost here and never emerge again. Dilya had managed to get them admitted past the front room; something about garnering the most attention.

They entered archives that seemed to expand forever beneath the streets of DC. "Five million maps," he barely managed to breathe it out.

"Sixty thousand atlas, rare globes, three thousand 3D models of terrain, and so much more." The librarian, a slight woman who had only recently taken on managing the collection, either didn't know of Miss Watson or was better at hiding it than the previous two.

"I'm definitely coming back here," he told Dilya. "Just imagine what I could learn about Mount Washington."

"Why that spot in particular?" the librarian asked in her soft voice. She was the very model of a librarian.

He pointed to the symbol on his sweatshirt. A simple mechanical gear and the words *Cog Railway*. "I'm learning to be a driver for them."

The librarian made quick use of a nearby terminal, then led them through the football field-sized area of tall metal cases, filled with big drawers to keep maps flat. Deep in the field, they dodged toward the sidelines. At a gray steel case exactly like every other around it, the librarian pulled on powder-free nitrile gloves and opened the third drawer down.

She flipped through the maps and finally extracted one from deep in the stack. With great care, she spread it out on a nearby table, then stepped back for him to discover it himself.

"It's—" The words stuck in his throat.

"*Initial survey of and a detailed assessment regarding the proposed route for a cog railway along the trail earlier established by Mister Ethan Allen Crawford upon the southwest face of Mount Washington in Coos County in the State of New Hampshire,*" Dilya read out. "It's dated 1852. That's one heck of a title."

Jimmy hadn't seen anything like it. And he'd wager that no one on the Cog Railway had either.

"If I can get a copy of this, it would make me immensely popular." Jimmy wished he could touch it. Could feel the markings that Sylvester Marsh had made a hundred and seventy years ago as he'd hiked on Mount Washington and dreamed of opening the peak for everyone to enjoy with a cog-driven railroad. It connected

Jimmy to the mountain more tightly, as if he was meant to be here in this moment.

"Easily done." The librarian rolled it carefully and carried it to the front area.

Minutes later, they were back on the street with a full-sized copy rolled into a stout cardboard tube.

"I'm sorry, Dilya. I'm know it was a delay, but this is incredible."

"You love it there, don't you? In New Hampshire."

"I do!" Only after he said it did he wish he'd been less emphatic. It wouldn't be any less true, but Dilya's life lay here, in Washington DC, not in the New Hampshire woods.

After that, she remained unusually silent, even by her standards. She only spoke during what was weirdly turning into routine at each successive library.

At the Folger Library, she met briefly with the librarian overseeing the largest collection of Shakespeare works and references anywhere in the world. His reaction *implied* that if he had indeed ever *heard* of a Miss Watson that such *hypothetical* knowledge would regrettably be neither current nor useful.

Dilya, sharing her close relationship with Miss Watson, did nothing to open that particular door any wider.

Jimmy considered faking an interest, but he and his dad, even Mom before she was killed, were more *The Bourne Identity* sort of people than *Much Ado About Nothing* people. In the end he left well enough alone and followed Dilya once more onto the street.

If she wasn't going to break the silence, he would. "What are we doing, anyway? I still don't understand her message. Visit a bunch of libraries then—"

"My best guess is that we're trying to attract attention. We're bait."

"We're *what?*" Jimmy twisted around to see if they were being followed.

"Don't!" Dilya grabbed his hand before he turned fully around. "No one has picked up our trail yet, but we have to keep trying."

"How do you know? Uh, never mind." Because if anyone knew, it would be Dilya, not him.

He focused forward as they headed west from the libraries and hit the National Mall. He pointed. "I was always more of a National Air and Space Museum sort than the places Miss Watson is leading us."

"I bet that you'll like the next one."

She hadn't let go of his hand, which only made it all the more confusing. There was no future that connected upstate New Hampshire and DC. Not that he planned to let go of her hand anytime soon.

Halfway back to the White House, they passed the US Secret Service headquarters building. Except they didn't pass it. At the far end, Dilya led him through one of the big glass doors into the interior.

8

"GOOD MORNING, MISS STEVENSON. WHAT CAN I DO FOR YOU today?"

Dilya ignored Jimmy's shock as she greeted the receptionist. It looked as if she might even be enjoying the moment at his expense. Did *everyone* in DC know her? How far out of his league was she?

"We'd like to speak with the ink librarian, if we may."

"The what?" Jimmy whispered, but the receptionist was already dialing.

Moments later the receptionist had signed them in, then pointed. "Take the elevator to the fifth floor. Do not let *him* speak to anyone or should I arrange an escort? Can he keep quiet?"

Since she was looking at him as he slipped the lanyard of the visitor's badge over his head, he replied with a simple, "Understood, ma'am."

When the elevator arrived and the door opened, Dilya squealed like, well, a girl, and threw herself at the person exiting into the lobby.

She'd wrapped her arms around a massive black man who towered above her.

"Hey there, Little One." His whisper was kind but inside of the first second, his surprise at Dilya's effusive greeting had shifted—to fully focus on Jimmy.

"Mr. Martin," the greeting offered no hint of his thoughts.

"Mr. Adams." Jimmy couldn't believe that Frank Adams knew his name. He was sure they'd never met. The man fit Dilya's stories too perfectly for there to be any question as to his identity. A towering black dude who could make you want to shrivel up and hide with a simple glance. Had Dilya told the head of the former President's Protection Detail all about Jimmy? He couldn't imagine why she would, yet Adams knew him.

"You two have met?" Dilya looked up at the towering man.

"Read his file after I saw this morning's flag that he entered the White House with you last night."

"The flag?"

He looked down at Dilya. "You think I don't know every time you step out of my White House? You went AWOL from the President's entourage in Tennessee five days ago and have been covering some interesting ground since. Do *not,*" he held up a finger that looked as big around as Dilya's wrist, "be thinking of telling me you simply wanted to catch up with your old Chef's Club pals."

Dilya, who had opened her mouth, now closed it. She glanced at Jimmy, but he could offer no more than a shrug.

"I, uh, lost someone."

"Looks like you found him." Frank flashed a brief grin over at Jimmy. He attempted to return it, but imagined that it came out more sickly than pleased. Then Frank crossed his arms, telling Dilya that she wasn't going anywhere until she was a whole lot clearer.

After yet another long pause, she whispered, "Miss Watson."

It wasn't as if they hadn't touted her name all over DC's libraries this morning.

Frank's expression went dark. "You *lost* her?"

Dilya nodded. Frank's gaze flicked to him as if Jimmy was some authority. He could only nod.

"Well, shit."

"You knew about her?" Jimmy thought nobody did.

"She was in my White House, Mr. Martin. I didn't bother her, but don't I know something saved our asses a couple times when nothing should have. Her being gone is *not* good news. What can you tell me?"

Dilya dug the translated code out of her back pocket and handed it to Frank.

He read it quickly but returned it slowly. "I'd best let you two get on with it. Little One, you have my number."

"On speed dial, Frank."

"Damn right. I'll fill in Beat, but she's at the UN New York for a meeting that, ah, included one of your Chef's Club." And with no further ceremony he walked off.

When Dilya didn't move, Jimmy pressed the call button for the elevator.

She kept turning to look in the direction Frank had departed.

"Don't you trust him? You sure acted like you do."

"The way he just left was odd and I'm wondering what he's up to. He and Beatrice are sort of my third set of parents. They'd take a bullet for me, I guess."

Jimmy suddenly wished he was back in New Hampshire. He didn't want to be in DC where someone might *have to* take a bullet to protect Dilya. He didn't want to live in a place where mothers were gunned down by a drunk wife when the cops restrained the husband beating her. He didn't want any part of murdered librarians and missing master spies.

Which meant he didn't want to be any part of Dilya's life either.

And that thought royally sucked.

9

DILYA WAS SURE THAT THE SECRET SERVICE INK LIBRARY would fascinate Jimmy. He barely reacted at all.

Their shelves held sixteen thousand samples of ink, markers, printer toner, and everything else used for writing over most of the last hundred years. Handling over five hundred cases a year, the librarians here investigated everything from counterfeit money to signatures forged with the wrong kind of ink. They'd helped crack cases like the DC Sniper in 2002 by the ink he left on the Tarot cards he used to claim each kill.

She and Jimmy then visited the US Mint, National Postal Museum, and the US Forest Service. The EPA was a little creepy. The number of Superfund sites in desperate need of clean up from toxic dumping or manufacturing was staggering.

She persevered and visited every special librarian she could think of. There were a ton of academic and corporate ones as well. They oversaw special collections from museums to the White House, wrote the indexes at the backs of books, and tracked everything from the medals issued to soldiers from every war all the way back to the Revolution to the progress of genetics research.

Dilya timed it so that they were back at the White House at noon to pick up her car. The CIA headquarters lay ten miles away in Langley, Virginia. Miss Watson had said to go there last.

She didn't think it was necessary as someone had picked up their trail while talking to the head librarian for the Marine Corps Band. The librarian stationed at the Marine Barracks in Southeast DC knew nothing of Miss Watson and had never been to the White House except for performances, but was so incredibly excited to show them through his the band's history and their music collection that she hadn't had the heart to brush him off.

The tail was felt not seen, but Miss Watson had trained her too well to mistrust that instinct. She considered alerting Jimmy. It might be safer, but she didn't want to spook their shadow as it would defeat what she guessed was the purpose of the entire morning.

Her exhaustion ran core deep. Not just because she'd slept three hours and then spent the next six visiting libraries all over DC. It was because Jimmy had barely said a word in the last three hours.

She'd tried talking to him about dog training, but not even that engaged him. When she suggested he could wait in her room, he'd roused himself enough to refuse. It was just as well, she wasn't sure how security would feel about him being there alone.

The drive out to the CIA campus turned painfully silent.

The dogs felt it too. Shelties were a very active breed. They wouldn't play as long as a Golden Retriever, nor were they as non-stop hyper as a Malinois, but they never ever drooped. Zackie and Merle curled up on opposite sides of the back seat for the drive.

The CIA's library and museum was no more public than many of the ones she'd been to today, but again her White House, Yankee White clearance opened even these doors. Though it certainly hadn't budged the librarian who had regarded their standard question with a grim glower. It radiated his hatred that they were permitted to intrude upon his hallowed ground.

She made a point of ambling through the historic exhibits they were permitted into. The more modern ones lay in an area restricted to active agents only, perhaps for training purposes.

Jimmy had reengaged a little, but the exhibit had ended just as it became interesting with the end of the Cold War. In the library itself, she recognized a large number of titles from Miss Watson's collection. For a few minutes she wondered if the CIA had snatched her collection and inserted it into their own. But then she began finding gaps. Their Russian language originals section of tradecraft was pitiful; Dilya had honed her limited childhood Russian to fluency on Miss Watson's books and knew it well.

"Why are we lingering here so long?"

Dilya considered. Jimmy might have gone silent, but he'd stuck by her. And she had some guesses as to what might happen next. If she was right, it would be unfair to Jimmy to let him follow her in blind.

"Exactly as Miss Watson predicted. Someone is tailing us."

Despite her expectations, Jimmy didn't spin around to scan behind them. "I figured that out for myself."

"How? I haven't actually seen the tail yet though I'm sure someone is there."

"I watched *you,* Dilya. You slowed down by half after the music soldier."

"They're Marines, not soldiers. Don't ever call them that unless you want to pick a fight."

"Okay. So why are we going even slower here?"

Dilya half smiled. "I thought I was delaying the inevitable a little bit for your sake, but now I'm not so sure. I've spent half my life studying this," she waved a hand at the library that surrounded them. "It always seemed so important. Now it feels..." she shrugged her shoulders but the itch of a target between her shoulder blades didn't go away.

Now that she'd come to a stop, Zackie laid down across her toes.

"It's never felt this real before. And I don't think I like it. I watched my parents die. At least you were spared that with your mom."

Jimmy started to protest but she quieted him with a touch. She liked how easily they communicated.

"Trust me. Imagining it the thousand ways you probably have, it's still less awful than the reality."

Jimmy rested his hand over hers on his arm and clasped it tightly.

She liked that too. "The real danger starts when we leave here."

"Figured that out for myself too."

"And you're sure you want to see it through to the end?"

"With you? Yes."

And there was the answer nothing in her life had prepared her for. *With her?* She'd always felt it was her alone against the world. But what if she wasn't?

10

THE REGISTRATION DESK WAS UNMANNED EXCEPT FOR A BOX with a handwritten sign *Leave Badges Here.* Even as they watched, a group leaving the conference stripped off their name badge holders and tossed them into the box on their way out the door.

Jimmy walked up and shuffled through the box for a moment, dredging up two badges. "I guess you're Cheryl unless you'd rather be Ursula. And I'm, oh wait, here's a James. That's close enough."

He kept *Cheryl's* hand in his as they entered the conference. A few remaining posters said this was the last day of the Special Library Association's annual conference.

Jimmy wanted to smack his forehead. Miss Watson's coded message had said to go to the CIA library last. *Then meet me at SLA trade 1pm.* Before today he'd never heard of Special Librarians, but he'd had a morning's masterclass in what they were.

And while he'd bet the booths were different, Comic-Cons had massive trade*show* floors selling signed books, costumes, and light sabers.

That meant Miss Watson was here somewhere. And they'd dragged a tail, other than the two belonging to their Shelties, straight to her. Exactly as Miss Watson had planned like they were pieces in her 3D chess game.

For a brief moment he wished he'd taken Dilya up on her offer to leave him at the White House. But even though there was no hope for them to be together, some part of him hadn't given up. Holding her last night as they slept. Holding her hand now. He wanted more of that not less.

Past the entry doors, Jimmy couldn't believe what he was seeing. It blew away every concept he'd ever had about librarians.

Groups of them lounged in comfortable sitting areas talking intently. Others filtered in and out of rooms that must have different lectures occurring. And yet more stood in the halls chatting in twos and threes. None of that was odd.

The weirdness was the variety.

Despite it being the last afternoon of a multi-day conference, some still wore immaculate business suits and dresses. But these were in the minority. Jeans and t-shirts were common. Earth mothers wearing wild batik muumuus mixed with goth-clad guys and Hawaiian-shirt-and-board-shorts-clad women wearing flip-flops or Birkenstocks. It was like they'd let all of the crazy ones out of their book-caves and put them in one place.

Overheard snatches of their conversation came peppered with words that sounded as if he should understand them, but he'd wager he was wrong: adjacency, false drops, expanders, and grey literature. He almost stopped to ask about that one but Dilya tugged him toward a pair of double doors standing wide open as if none of this was foreign to her.

The doors admitted them to a mid-sized ballroom. It wasn't like a Comic-Con with its vast spread of booths, sometimes filling multiple convention center ballrooms. Instead there were fifty or so tables. Some displayed software, others advertised binding and restoration, yet others consulting services. The SLA had a large table, as did National Public Radio—they hadn't made it to NPR's library. There were *Now-hiring* headhunters, and he spotted the Western Association of Map Librarians. In a different life he could be at that table himself.

He stopped at the ASME desk. Though he was a member of the American Society of Mechanical Engineers, he'd never thought about their library. He could have talked to them for hours but he wasn't a librarian nor had he paid for the conference, so he kept it brief but couldn't help smiling as they moved on.

Dilya led them halfway around the room before pausing at the Oxford University Press Table. She pointed at the floor and Zackie sat tight against her left leg. Merle looked at her, then at Zackie, then at him. Jimmy tried jabbing a finger toward the floor with equal authority. He wasn't sure which of them, he or Merle was more surprised when his dog sat at his side.

The person behind the table was busy chatting with another librarian.

With her free hand, Dilya picked up a copy of *Hacker, Influencer, Faker, Spy: Intelligence Agencies in the Digital Age.* She freed her other hand from his and began turning the pages. Jimmy would far rather be reading the latest issue of the *Journal of Applied Mechanics* that he'd snagged from the ASME table.

There had to be some way that two people from such different worlds could—

"He's in," Dilya said in a perfectly normal voice, one that didn't draw anyone's attention except his.

Jimmy resisted looking toward the door, instead doing his best to appear interested in the true implications of a cyber war. He'd played enough online war games in high school for that to majorly creep him out. When he couldn't stand it any longer, Jimmy looked around the room.

There was a casual ebb and flow. He'd seen it at the Comic-Cons he'd been to. The last day, nothing happened too quickly. Everyone was run down but reluctant to leave before they absolutely had to.

He didn't see any anomalies. Everyone belonged here except themselves.

"You sure?"

"I didn't watch directly, but I saw a break in the traffic flow by the door. Then they blended in. Trust me. He, she, or they are here."

Or *they*? He hadn't considered that. He'd figured that Dilya could protect them from one bad guy, but multiple? This wasn't something he had any training in.

"Any sign of Miss W?"

Dilya shook her head. "But then she can look like anything she wants."

For half an hour, they stopped at one table after another. Jimmy got the hang of pretending he was a software geek looking for a job. Since the only untrue part of that was any desire to change jobs, he could play it well. Dilya's fascination with printed books in every form also worked well.

They were deep in the middle of the room when Zackie's head popped up. She began scanning around. Her nose had picked up some scent. But since her eyes were level with people's knees, there wasn't much for her to see. Merle was looking as well, but only because Zackie was doing so.

"Dilya?" he asked to draw her attention to her dog.

"She's here. Let's go." Dilya snapped her fingers to get Zackie's attention, then flashed a sign as she whispered, "*Faigh.*"

"What's that one?"

"It means *seek* or *fetch.* It switches her mode and all she'll care about now is finding a familiar scent. I didn't train her on explosives, but rather on people. She picked up the scent of someone she knows, so I'm hoping she leads us to Miss Watson."

And indeed Zackie set off in the lead. They went up the middle aisle. At the end of the row, she veered right toward the entry door then veered left so suddenly that Jimmy almost tripped over her.

Halfway down the back aisle, as far as possible from the exit door, Dilya whispered without quite looking up, "The scarf. It's her knitting."

There was no question who she was talking about. A tall woman with sunlight bright blonde hair and an impeccable business suit, the kind that always looked so good in magazine ads, wore an incongruous scarf—wide with bright color bands that reached her knees. "That's Tom Baker's Doctor Who scarf."

"Who?"

"Exactly," he half hoped they'd slip into the old Abbot and Costello *Who's on First?* routine so that he didn't scream to release his nerves.

He remembered Miss Watson as a small hunched woman in her seventies or eighties, not this magazine-ad model in her forties wearing a crazy scarf. So, Dilya and Zackie had tracked Miss Watson's *scent* to this woman's scarf.

Mere feet from the woman, Zackie turned to look back the direction they'd come from and let out a happy yip.

11

SOMETHING SLAMMED JIMMY ASIDE—HARD.

He crashed into a table, knocking aside dozens of copies of children's board books before upending the table itself onto the two elderly women seated behind it.

Dilya! She'd shoved hard against his shoulder, driving him out of the aisle—plummeting to the floor out of harm's way. He saw her swing her arm down and a black folding knife dropped into her palm. She snapped it open with a practiced flick.

The blonde in the scarf remained perfectly still as a man in khakis and a black dress shirt eased toward her along the aisle from close behind his and Dilya's positions. He ignored Jimmy and Dilya as if they were of no consequence.

From his vantage sprawled on the floor, Jimmy saw the man cock his hand back like Spiderman ready to throw a sticky web. Then he recalled an exhibit in the CIA's Cold War museum. A gun that strapped onto the underside of a person's forearm. When fired, the hand had to be raised to not shoot your own fingers. Gun or poison dart, deadly either way.

He had it raised halfway to the blonde's chest but he hesitated. With an upstroke of her arm, Dilya's jabbed her knife deep into his forearm. The man screamed as blood poured out of the wound.

Zackie jumped up high enough to clamp a hard bite on the man's injured arm. When he moved to strike at Zackie, Merle latched onto his crotch, which elicited another scream.

A woman as dark as Dilya, though several inches shorter and more seriously built, stepped up behind the man. With no hint of mercy, she sent the man crashing facedown onto the floor mere inches from Jimmy.

He rolled aside to avoid the blood pouring from his arm.

The woman held him pinned there with a boot on the back of his neck as she searched him for other weapons.

The blonde in the scarf knelt down and zip-tied his hands and feet.

And one of the older women behind the table struggled to her feet—Miss Watson! She reached out to pet Zackie, who nudged her shin.

Then she looked down at the man. "Carlo." She casually rested a foot on his bloody forearm, making the man whimper. "Now tell me who sent you after all these years."

12

FOR ALL OF THE TRAINING SHE'D HAD, INCLUDING GROWING UP in a war zone, Dilya had never actually hurt someone before.

Carlo screamed his pain and fury as Miss Watson questioned him and Emily Beale knelt on his back to keep him pinned.

Dilya could only bury her face in Kee's shoulder.

Her stepmom held her close and stroked her hair. "I'm so glad you texted me yesterday, Dilyana." Her whisper was too soft to carry beyond Dilya's own ears but hearing her full name felt like a wake-up call, as if a memory had suddenly jostled her. A memory of...Jimmy saying her true name. And while trying to be angry that he'd discovered it, realizing that she liked the sound of it coming from him.

She forced herself to look back at the scene.

There'd been some additional screams from those who'd witnessed the moment but those rapidly subsided.

Now the tableau had changed.

The man still lay facedown on the floor with a white handkerchief turned red with blood bound around his arm.

The tall blonde, who Zackie had recognized, held an impressive array of weapons. As she handed the massive scarf back to Miss Watson, Dilya spotted the edge of the bulletproof vest Emily Beale wore under her elegant jacket.

As she and Jimmy had left the Cog Railway forever and twenty-four hours ago, she'd sent two texts. The first to her stepmom and the second to Emily Beale at her Montana ranch. She knew that she could rely on them to handle any situation. They were the two most dangerous women she'd ever met.

Frank Adams stepped into the room. He picked out the disturbance before his second foot made it through the doorway. Two other agents followed him over.

"Is it done?"

Emily smiled at him. "Your timing is perfect as always."

His grunt at the jibe didn't sound pleased. Another story Dilya didn't know and would have to ferret out of them—some other day.

Frank picked up the prone man by the scruff of his neck as if he weighed less than a Sheltie dog. He shook him once—hard—then tossed him to the two other agents and waved them away. "What am I charging him on?"

Miss Watson stepped forward. "Five counts of murder, the details are already in your email inbox, and the attempted murder of Major Beale while posing as me."

Frank blew out a sharp breath as he squared off to face Miss Watson. "So, the mystery lady has emerged from the basement."

Miss Watson tipped her head graciously. "By the way, you'll want to have a chat with the President. The new head of the Russia Desk at the CIA is the one behind the murders. Carlo's talents were engaged against US citizens on US soil—which breaks every CIA rule, in an attempt to hide a dirty past of the Russia Desk. He knew that *I* knew about that past. I stayed in one place too long and rumors of my existence leaked out. Discovering I still lived, he came hunting me—assassinating my peer group of librarians as he tried to trace me. I'll also send you the recording I just made of Carlo fingering him."

Frank's smile promised full retribution. "Consider it done." Then he scrubbed a hand in Dilya's hair—the only person to ever get away with that—and strode away before she could bat at his hand.

Miss Watson led them all to a quiet corner of the room before turning to her. "Thank you, my dear. Calling in your second mother and Emily was very well done. I'm glad you learned the lesson I so failed at, to seek the help of others when needed."

Dilya barely managed a nod. She could still feel every moment of stabbing Carlo in the arm. The slip of the blade as it impacted the hidden arm-gun. Then, as the razor-sharp tanto point slid into flesh and impacted bone, twisting it to drive it deep into his wrist tendons to disable his attack.

Emily used a water bottle from a nearby table to rinse off her knife over a handy garbage can, then folded it closed and held it out.

Dilya shook her head. She never wanted to see it again.

Emily grabbed her wrist, pushed up her sleeve to expose the sheath, and slid in the knife. Without letting go, she looked down at her with those perfect blue eyes. "You did what was necessary, no more. I couldn't have done it better myself."

Dilya wanted to turn away.

Ever since she'd first met Emily, as a terrified orphan refugee meeting the Army's best attack helicopter pilot, she'd wanted to be like her. "How...?" but she couldn't form the question. How did women like Emily, like her second mom Kee, kill people?

Being Emily, of course she had no problem reading Dilya's expression. "By never becoming used to it. I still feel every single one. And I can only hope that the world is a better place for each of those I or my team took down."

Kee was nodding her agreement.

Emily patted the knife now hidden against Dilya's wrist one last time as if confirming that's where it belonged—and how could Dilya ever argue with Emily—then turned to Miss Watson. "Any plans? Returning to the White House basement?"

Miss Watson now stood almost as tall as Emily. She'd been a great beauty in her youth and it still showed. Her hair had come loose and now hung in a silver cascade past her shoulders. "I was thinking about finding a place in the sunlight after all these years hidden away."

"I happen to know a nice ranch in Montana. You'd be more than welcome."

"That, my dear, is one of the nicest offers I've ever had. None better since Dilya agreed to let me teach her eight years ago." Her nod accepted the invitation, then she glanced at Dilya. "There remains the final disposition of my library."

Dilya didn't know what to say. If she took over the library of Miss Watson's tradecraft books, then she'd be setting herself on a path that would only lead to more situations like this one—or worse. But she'd spent so long training for this, much of it without realizing, that she didn't know where else to turn.

It was the obvious choice. So why was it churning her stomach into knots?

Then a hard slid down her hair before tucking around her waist.

"Super wicked über *extra* cool, Dilyana," Jimmy whispered for her alone.

She'd peripherally been aware of him righting tables, calming people, rearranging scattered books and flyers. The geeky boy had turned into a geeky man who was good with people and knew what he wanted. Far more than she did.

And one of the things he wanted was *her*.

New Hampshire. What might await her there?

She remembered last year's conference at the Bretton Woods Resort close by the Cog Railway. Remembered the Secret Service agent and her dog who had saved hundreds of lives there, then retired to become their new head of security. Perhaps she'd like an assistant.

Dilya looked at the three women awaiting her: Kee, Emily, and Miss Watson. Each had filled such a huge role in her life. Yet each had traveled along such different paths—shooter, pilot, and spy now turned stepmother, friend, and mentor.

She looked up at Jimmy. Patient and doing his best to hide any sadness from her. Hiding it for *her* sake.

She'd *felt* safe since the first moment Kee had rescued her long before she became Dilya's stepmom. She'd *felt* when Carlo had picked up their trail. And now she *felt* ready to choose her own path as they had.

Dilya looked down at Zackie and Merle, who were lying across her and Jimmy's toes, and couldn't help smiling. When she looked back up, all three women were smiling at her as if they had read her decision before she knew it herself. Read it and approved.

"I think that what I need to do next," she looked at Jimmy, "is go train a dog in New Hampshire."

"Really?" Jimmy cried out as he tried to spin her to fully face him. But both of them had twenty pounds of Sheltie lying across their toes and ended up tumbling to the conference floor. On the convention floor of the Special Librarians Association was a weird place for their first kiss. She could think of many worse places to be, but not many better ones.

Ignoring the two dogs happily attempting to join in did cause some problems though.

END NOTE

REGRETTABLY, I WAS UNABLE TO LOCATE SYLVESTER MARSH'S survey map in the Library of Congress database of their collection, if there ever was one. However, as they do still possess a number of as yet uncataloged maps, I continue to have hopes.

On that note, my amazing research librarian wife found these, which might amuse:

For a deep dive, there's a book titled *Sylvester Marsh and the Cog Railway*.

The 1894 Railroad Map of New Hampshire, which *does* include the Mount Washington Cog Railway. However, it is mislabeled as still belonging to the Concord and Montreal Railroad though it had been transferred to the Boston & Maine Railroad in 1889 (note the detail section showing the Cog Railway line itself).

http://www.old-maps.com/nh/nhs_1894_Railroad.htm

———

*If you enjoyed this story
please consider leaving a review.
They really help.*

Keep reading for an exciting excerpt from:
White House Protection Force #1: *Off the Leash*

AFTERWORD

If you enjoyed this
please consider leaving a review.
They really help.

Keep reading for an exciting excerpt from
The Secret Service Dogs:
Off the Leash

Be sure to visit:
https://mlbuchman.com/fan-club-freebies

- *Bonus Scene/Story for the novels*
- *Recipes from the books*
- *Character list, place maps, plane pictures, and more*

OFF THE LEASH (EXCERPT)

IF YOU ENJOYED THAT, YOU'LL LOVE
THIS TALE!

OFF THE LEASH (EXCERPT)

"You're joking."

"Nope. That's his name. And he's yours now."

Sergeant Linda Hamlin wondered quite what it would take to wipe that smile off Lieutenant Jurgen's face. A 120mm round from an M1A1 Abrams Main Battle Tank came to mind.

The kennel master of the US Secret Service's Canine Team was clearly a misogynistic jerk from the top of his polished head to the bottoms of his equally polished boots. She wondered if the shoelaces were polished as well.

Then she looked over at the poor dog sitting hopefully on the concrete kennel floor. His stall had a dog bed three times his size and a water bowl deep enough for him to bathe in. No toys, because toys always came from the handler as a reward. He offered her a sad sigh and a liquid doggy gaze. The kennel even smelled wrong, more of sanitizer than dog. The walls seemed to echo with each bark down the long line of kennels housing the candidate hopefuls for the next addition to the Secret Service's team.

Thor—really?—was a brindle-colored mutt, part who-knew and part no-one-cared. He looked like a cross between an oversized, long-haired schnauzer and a dust mop that someone had spilled dark gray paint on. After mixing in streaks of tawny brown, they'd left one white paw just to make him all the more laughable.

And of course Lieutenant Jerk Jurgen would assign Thor to the first woman on the USSS K-9 team.

Unable to resist, she leaned over far enough to scruff the dog's ears. He was the physical opposite of the sleek and powerful Malinois MWDs—military war dogs—that she'd been handling for the 75th Rangers for the last five years. They twitched with eagerness and nerves. A good MWD was seventy pounds of pure drive—every damn second of the day. If the mild-mannered Thor weighed thirty pounds, she'd be surprised. And he looked like a little girl's best friend who should have a pink bow on his collar.

Jurgen was clearly ex-Marine and would have no respect for the Army. Of course, having been in the Army's Special Operations Forces, she knew better than to respect a Marine.

"We won't let any old swabbie bother us, will we?"

Jurgen snarled—definitely Marine Corps. Swabbie was slang for a Navy sailor and a Marine always took offense at being lumped in with them no matter how much they belonged. Of course the swabbies took offense at having the Marines lumped with *them*. Too bad there weren't any Navy around so that she could get two for the price of one. Jurgen wouldn't be her boss, so appeasing him wasn't high on her to-do list.

At least she wouldn't need any of the protective bite gear working with Thor. With his stature, he was an explosives detection dog without also being an attack one.

"Where was he trained?" She stood back up to face the beast.

"Private outfit in Montana—some place called Henderson's Ranch. Didn't make their MWD program," his scoff said exactly what he thought the likelihood of any dog outfit in Montana being worthwhile. "They wanted us to try the little runt out."

She'd never heard of a training program in Montana. MWDs all came out of Lackland Air Force Base training. The Secret Service mostly trained their own and they all came from Vohne Liche Kennels in Indiana. Unless... Special Operations Forces dogs were trained by private contractors. She'd worked beside a Delta Force dog for a single month—he'd been incredible.

"Is he trained in English or German?" Most American MWDs were trained in German so that there was no confusion in case a command word happened to be part of a spoken sentence. It also made it harder for any random person on the battlefield to shout something that would confuse the dog.

"German according to his paperwork, but he won't listen to me much in either language."

Might as well give the diminutive Thor a few basic tests. A snap of her fingers and a slap on her thigh had the dog dropping into a smart "heel" position. No need to call out *Fuss*—*by my foot.*

"*Pass auf!*" *Guard!* She made a pistol with her thumb and forefinger and aimed it at Jurgen as she grabbed her forearm with her other hand—the military hand sign for enemy.

The little dog snarled at Jurgen sharply enough to have him backing out of the kennel. "Goddamn it!"

"*Ruhig.*" *Quiet.* Thor maintained his fierce posture but dropped the snarl.

"*Gute Hund.*" *Good dog,* Linda countered the command.

Thor looked up at her and wagged his tail happily. She tossed him a doggie treat, which he caught midair and crunched happily.

She didn't bother looking up at Jurgen as she knelt once more to check over the little dog. His scruffy fur was so soft that it tickled. Good strength in the jaw, enough to show he'd had bite training despite his size—perfect if she ever needed to take down a three-foot-tall terrorist. Legs said he was a jumper.

"Take your time, Hamlin. I've got nothing else to do with the rest of my goddamn day except babysit you and this mutt."

"Is the course set?"

"Sure. Take him out," Jurgen's snarl sounded almost as nasty as Thor's before he stalked off.

She stood and slapped a hand on her opposite shoulder.

Thor sprang aloft as if he was attached to springs and she caught him easily. He'd cleared well over double his own height. Definitely trained...and far easier to catch than seventy pounds of hyperactive Malinois.

She plopped him back down on the ground. On lead or off? She'd give him the benefit of the doubt and try off first to see what happened.

Linda zipped up her brand-new USSS jacket against the cold and led the way out of the kennel into the hard sunlight of the January morning.

Keep reading now!
A great tale of romance and adventure,

Off the Leash (excerpt)

Of dogs, chocolates, and villains.
Available at fine retailers everywhere.
Off the Leash

And please don't forget that review for
The Disappearance Cipher

ABOUT THE AUTHOR

USA TODAY AND AMAZON #1 BESTSELLER M. L. "MATT" Buchman started writing on a flight south from Japan to ride his bicycle across the Australian Outback. Just part of a solo around-the-world trip that ultimately launched his writing career.

From the very beginning, his powerful female heroines insisted on putting character first, *then* a great adventure. He's since written over 75 action-adventure thrillers and military romantic suspense novels. And more than 200 short stories, and a fast-growing pile of read-by-author audiobooks.

PW declares of his Miranda Chase action-adventure thrillers: "Tom Clancy fans open to a strong female lead will clamor for more." About his military romantic thrillers: "Like Robert Ludlum and Nora Roberts had a book baby."

His fans say: "I want more now...of everything!" That his characters are even more insistent than his fans is a hoot. He is also the founder and editor of *Thrill Ride – the Magazine*.

As a 30-year project manager with a geophysics degree

who has designed and built houses, flown and jumped out of planes, and solo-sailed a 50' ketch, he is awed by what is possible. He and his wife presently live on the North Shore of Massachusetts. More at: www.mlbuchman.com.

Other works by M. L. Buchman: *(* - also in audio)*

Action-Adventure Thrillers

Dead Chef
One Chef!
Two Chef!

Miranda Chase
Drone*
Thunderbolt*
Condor*
Ghostrider*
Raider*
Chinook*
Havoc*
White Top*
Start the Chase*
Lightning*
Skibird*
Nightwatch*
Osprey*
Gryphon*

Science Fiction / Fantasy

Deities Anonymous
Cookbook from Hell: Reheated
Saviors 101

Contemporary Romance

Eagle Cove
Return to Eagle Cove
Recipe for Eagle Cove
Longing for Eagle Cove
Keepsake for Eagle Cove

Love Abroad
Heart of the Cotswolds: England
Path of Love: Cinque Terre, Italy

Where Dreams
Where Dreams are Born
Where Dreams Reside
Where Dreams Are of Christmas*
Where Dreams Unfold
Where Dreams Are Written
Where Dreams Continue

Non-Fiction

Strategies for Success
Managing Your Inner Artist/Writer
Estate Planning for Authors*
Character Voice
Narrate and Record Your Own
Audiobook*
Beyond Prince Charming: One Guy's
Guide to Writing Men in Romance

Short Story Series by M. L. Buchman:

Action-Adventure Thrillers

Dead Chef

Miranda Chase Stories

Romantic Suspense

Antarctic Ice Fliers

US Coast Guard

Contemporary Romance

Eagle Cove

Other

Deities Anonymous (fantasy)

Single Titles

The Emily Beale Universe
(military romantic suspense)

The Night Stalkers
MAIN FLIGHT
The Night Is Mine
I Own the Dawn
Wait Until Dark
Take Over at Midnight
Light Up the Night
Bring On the Dusk
By Break of Day
Target of the Heart
Target Lock on Love
Target of Mine
Target of One's Own
NIGHT STALKERS HOLIDAYS
*Daniel's Christmas**
*Frank's Independence Day**
*Peter's Christmas**
Christmas at Steel Beach
*Zachary's Christmas**
*Roy's Independence Day**
*Damien's Christmas**
Christmas at Peleliu Cove

Henderson's Ranch
*Nathan's Big Sky**
*Big Sky, Loyal Heart**
*Big Sky Dog Whisperer**
*Tales of Henderson's Ranch**

Shadow Force: Psi
*At the Slightest Sound**
*At the Quietest Word**
*At the Merest Glance**
*At the Clearest Sensation**

White House Protection Force
*Off the Leash**
*On Your Mark**
*In the Weeds**

Firehawks
Pure Heat
Full Blaze
*Hot Point**
*Flash of Fire**
Wild Fire
SMOKEJUMPERS
*Wildfire at Dawn**
*Wildfire at Larch Creek**
*Wildfire on the Skagit**

Delta Force
*Target Engaged**
*Heart Strike**
*Wild Justice**
*Midnight Trust**

Emily Beale Universe Short Story Series
The Night Stalkers
The Night Stalkers Stories
The Night Stalkers CSAR
The Night Stalkers Wedding Stories
The Future Night Stalkers

Delta Force
Th Delta Force Shooters
The Delta Force Warriors

Firehawks
The Firehawks Lookouts
The Firehawks Hotshots
The Firebirds

White House Protection Force
Stories

Future Night Stalkers
Stories (Science Fiction)

SIGN UP FOR M. L. BUCHMAN'S NEWSLETTER TODAY

and receive:
Release News
Free Short Stories
a Free Book

Get your free book today. Do it now.
free-book.mlbuchman.com